TRUCKERS

TRUCKERS
True Gay Erotica

EDITED BY JOHNNY HANSEN

CLEIS
PRESS

Published in the United States by Cleis Press Inc., P.O. Box 14697, San Francisco, California 94114.

Printed in the United States.
Cover design: Scott Idleman
Cover photograph: Thomas Watkin
Text design: Frank Wiedemann
Cleis logo art: Juana Alicia
First Edition.
10 9 8 7 6 5 4 3 2 1

Christopher Pierce's "Fucked at the Truck Stop" originally appeared in a slightly different form in *Straight? Volume 2* (Alyson Books, 2003). Simon Sheppard's "Gutpunch" originally appeared in a slightly different form in *Hotter than Hell: And Other Stories* (Alyson Books, 2001).

Contents

INTRODUCTION

Judging from trucking-world slang alone, you'd think all truckers were gay: big rubbers (twenty-four-inch tires), chicken coop (weigh station), hammer down (accelerate), meat wagon (ambulance), pickle park (rest stop), motion lotion (diesel fuel), and good buddy, for example. In fact, "good buddy," in trucker speak, has actually evolved into a derogatory term for "gay man."

Of course not all truckers are gay, but plenty of them (and in my fantasies, *most* of them!) love to stop for a quickie with a young truck-stop hustler now and then, or pick up a sweaty hitchhiker for a little no-strings-attached fucking and sucking.

The wild, true confessions of truckers about their sexual proclivities in this first-of-its-kind anthology are evidence to that. From hot and horny trucker studs getting nasty action in truck-stop showers, to lonesome married big-rig men turning discreet tricks with handsome strangers, to filthy rest-stop delights in the middle of nowhere, the men in this anthology bare all, revealing their sordid secrets and sexy details of life on—and off—the road.

So, tell me, good buddy, are you ready for one heck of a dirty, dusty, sweat-soaked ride? Well, buckle down, because the men in this collection are out to take you on a wild, hot, sex-filled road trip you'll never forget.

—Johnny Hansen

SUMMER TRUCKER

Hank Edwards

The summer I turned nineteen I got a job as a busboy at a crappy little truck-stop diner just outside my college town. I hated the job, the bitchy waitresses, the asshole owner, and most of the customers. There was one guy, however, who always nodded, smiled, and said hi to me.

He was a trucker named John, and he had the finest ass I had seen in a long time. He was just shy of six feet with a dark red flattop, trim red-gold beard, and green eyes. His favorite attire was faded blue jeans with old flannel shirts left unbuttoned over white tank tops, his red-gold chest hair peeking out above the top of the neckline.

John's schedule brought him by every other day around lunchtime, and I started to look for him. I liked watching him walk through the diner, his stride sure and fluid as his fine ass clenched and released inside his faded jeans. He had big hands flecked with the same red-gold hair that covered his chest and face, and I daydreamed about how those hands would feel running down my body, cupping my ass, or squeezing my cock. He must have asked one of the waitresses my name because one day he surprised me by saying, "Hey, Hank," as he headed for a booth. Hearing my name spoken in his deep, raspy voice made my cock stand on end, and I was glad to be holding the dish bin in front of me.

I spent a month at the diner, watching out the greasy windows as other people sped by on the highway to places I was sure I'd never see. Clive was chewing my ass, a daily occurrence, and I'd finally had enough. I untied my apron and threw it on the floor.

"I quit!" I shouted in his face, causing Clive to fall miraculously silent.

"Oh…oh, yeah?" he shouted at my back as I pushed through the door into the heat of the day. "Well, don't come sniffing around asking for your job back."

I paused to take a breath of humid air spiked with diesel fumes, then started out across the macadam parking lot. I had no idea what I was going to do for money. I just knew I didn't have to work for Clive, asshole extraordinaire, any longer.

"Hey!" someone shouted, and I turned, surprised to find John, my favorite customer, trotting toward me from the diner.

"Oh, hi," I said. "I didn't see you come in."

"Yeah, you were busy getting your ass chewed out by Clive." He put his hands in the pockets of his jeans. "Look, I heard you quit, and I don't blame you." He leaned close, and I caught a whiff of his scent: woody and subtle, tinged lightly with sweat. "The guy's been an asshole as long as I can remember."

We grinned at each other, and I nearly let out a sad moan when he leaned away again. "So, Hank, any idea what you're going to do?"

I shrugged. "Not really. I'm just staying with friends here this summer so I don't have a lease or anything. I was thinking I might bum around, see some of the country."

John nodded. "Yeah? Like a road trip or something?"

"Yeah, like that. But I don't have a car or anything." I looked over my shoulder at the highway. "Guess I could hitchhike."

John looked at the highway as well, thinking, then flicked his eyes back to me. "You wanna ride with me?"

I blinked at him. "Up to Marquette and back?" During one of our conversations I'd learned John made a run from Detroit to Marquette, delivering appliances to a couple of stores in the Upper Peninsula.

He shook his head. "I picked up a new route I'm starting today, to California and back."

My eyes widened. "California? Seriously?" I was at a loss, my mind spinning. "Um, shit, John, I don't know. It's a great offer, but we don't know each other that well and it's a long drive to California."

John shrugged. "So? That's what the drive's all about. Come on, you've got nothing going on, you said it yourself."

My mind latched on to the final resistance. "I only have about a hundred dollars."

John laughed. "Well, shit, that's a hundred more than me."

I took a deep breath, held it, then said, "Okay," with the exhalation.

John's smile lit up his whole face, and I thought if nothing else went right on the trip, just seeing that smile was enough.

"Great! Climb up in my rig and we'll stop by to get your stuff, then we'll hit the road."

When I climbed into the cab I was amazed how much room there was. Behind the driver and passenger seats lay a thick mattress covered in satin sheets and a bunch of pillows. Nets strung from the ceiling held his personal items, and a small cooler in the back corner housed his beverages. As John eased his truck onto the service road, I flipped off Clive, who stood watching from one of the diner's dirty windows.

At the flat where I was crashing with my friends, I ran through the place grabbing my clothes and personal effects, stuffing them in my duffel bag. I realized I had no clean underwear so I packed all the dirty pairs, figuring I could wash them in a Laundromat or a rest-stop sink down the road. I pulled on a pair of shorts with a T-shirt, left a hastily scribbled note, and trotted out the door to John's truck idling in the street. My stomach was knotted with the excitement of heading toward the unknown and doing so with John.

"Damn, that was quick," John said. He took my duffel bag and tossed it in the storage area in back then looked at me closely. "Okay, you're sure about this, right?"

I nodded. "Yeah, I'm sure. Let's go."

We hit the road and started talking, comparing our childhoods and family situations. I found out he was thirty-three, fourteen years older than me. We danced around the subject of relationships, both of us admitting to having had girlfriends but no serious involvements at the moment. I realized suddenly I wasn't sure John was gay and that maybe my whole impression of what the trip would involve could be wrong. He could just be a friendly, lonely straight guy who drove a truck and enjoyed the company of younger guys. Yeah, right.

We soon fell silent, both of us lost in our thoughts as the highway rolled beneath the truck's thick tires.

Later that night I was still unsure about John's orientation, and I didn't know how to ask. Guys didn't just hit on each other when I was nineteen. John slowed down and eased the truck into a rest area. He rolled to a stop in an area removed from the bathrooms and shut down the engine, then turned to me.

"I'm gonna take a leak," he said. "Then we can turn in for the night."

I checked my watch. "Turn in? It's only ten-thirty."

John nodded. "Yep, and we gotta be on the road by six to beat the morning rush in Kansas City." He grabbed his shaving kit and swung out of the cab, his flannel shirt billowing behind him like a superhero's cape.

I put my head back and let out a sigh. Images of John and me drinking at roadside bars and heading back to the truck for hot, sweaty sex evaporated. I really was just along to keep him company and watch the Midwest flatlands roll by. I dug for my toothbrush and climbed out of the cab to head for the restroom as well.

John was standing bare-chested at the sinks when I walked in the men's room, rinsing an armpit with a washcloth, and I couldn't help stopping to stare. A physical ache erupted in my groin as I imagined burying my face in the pale, hairy valley of his pit and shooting a hot load of cum across his flat stomach. He shot me a smile in the mirror, then pulled a handful of paper towels from the dispenser and dried off.

"See you back at the truck," he said as he slipped on his flannel shirt.

I brushed my teeth and washed up as well, using a wad of paper towels to wash my own pits. I considered taking the time to jerk off but decided against it, still harboring a secret desire that John would make a move when I returned to the truck.

I crossed the asphalt parking lot still releasing the heat of the day and opened the door to climb into the cab. John sat on the mattress in his underwear, his back against the wall of the cab and a bottle of Jack Daniel's snuggled against his crotch. My eyes dropped to the round, bulky package straining against the searing white cotton of his briefs. His hairy legs were long and strong, his bare feet long and pale, at least size elevens, the tops dusted with red-gold hair.

"Thirsty?" John asked, and passed me a plastic cup with a couple inches of Jack.

"Fuck, yeah," I said, downing the whiskey in a single gulp. Heat flared out from my stomach as the liquor hit me, and I closed my eyes, riding the wave. "Damn, that's good."

John snorted a laugh and poured me another. "Well, Hank, here's to living your dream of seeing the good ol' U.S. of A." He raised his cup, and we swallowed our whiskey. "Whew! That's good shit. Hey, go ahead and strip on down to your skivvies. It's going to be a little humid in here tonight what with both of us bunked down and all."

The whiskey had burned away all my tension, and I didn't hesitate for a moment. I pulled off my T-shirt, untied my basketball shoes, and peeled off my socks. Just as I yanked down my shorts and my boner sprang free I remembered I wasn't wearing underwear.

"Shit a brick," John muttered. The cup stopped at his lips and his eyes locked on my dick. "You don't waste any time, do you?"

"I'm sorry, I just... You're just so hot and I didn't have clean underwear and—"

He stopped my words with his mouth, his hand wrapping tight around my cock. My brain spun as his whiskey-laced tongue filled my mouth. His beard scratched my face while his hands grabbed and stroked my body.

In a moment I was kissing him back, our tongues battling for dominance. His fingers pinched my nipples hard, and I grunted into his mouth as he pulled me on top of him. One of us had pulled off John's briefs, but to this day I'm not sure if it was him or me. Either way, we were both nude as I lay atop him, our cocks grinding together, his hands kneading my ass-cheeks.

We kissed for what felt like hours, cocks smearing precum over our bellies and thighs. We rolled back and forth across his mattress, the satin sheets slipping beneath us, me on top for a time, then John, until finally he broke the embrace and rose up over me.

"You are too fucking hot," he said, his voice deep and dangerous.

"I bet you say that to all the busboys."

He grinned and kissed me again, his tongue slopping around my lips and chin. He moved lower, kissing my neck and sending fireworks blasting through my head. On his way down my body he stopped at my nipples, sucking and biting them into hard, dime-size points. His tongue slid lower, parting the brown chest hair over my stomach and dipping into my navel. I groaned and twitched underneath him, my hands running over his bristly flat-top and strong shoulders.

Moving lower still, he ran the tip of his tongue along my throbbing shaft. He took my balls in the palm of one big, strong hand and pulled them taut, then opened his mouth and swallowed me whole.

When it came to oral sex the few guys I'd been with in college didn't hold a candle to John. He knew what he was doing, and when he deep-throated me that first time I nearly shot my load in his throat. I groaned and gasped, my head thrashing back and forth while John sucked and slurped along my cock. I've got seven inches, and he worked each sensitive inch like he hadn't eaten for a week. He got me close to climax, so close, then eased up, waiting until I had calmed down only to get me worked up again.

Swinging his hips around, he straddled my head and let his thick cock dangle over my face. I grabbed it in my fist and stroked its length as I studied his meat. *This is John's cock,* I kept telling myself. *Those are John's balls. I'm finally fulfilling my fantasy.*

He was longer than me, and thicker, much thicker. I tugged and stroked his cock as he grunted and snuffed around my own dick still lodged in his throat. His balls were big and loose, shaved clean. I'd never seen a man with shaved balls before, and I ran my tongue over them. The taste of John's sweaty balls burst on my tongue, encouraging me to bury my nose in the sensitive spot between his balls and his asshole. I breathed in, drawing the sexy, honest smell of John's sweat into my nose and feeling my cock jump in his mouth.

He raised his head long enough to say, "Suck my cock," before he bent back to work on mine.

I started working on the head, sucking and slurping, running my tongue around the meaty, heart-shaped cap. In no time I was taking him deep in my throat, gagging a few times but eager to suck the cum right out of his balls. I tentatively rubbed a finger against the satiny wrinkle of his anus, and he groaned deep in his throat.

"Oh, yeah," he said. "Finger my ass. That's it, push it in."

I slid the tip of my finger in his ass to the first knuckle then pulled it out. Pushing it in again, deeper this time, brought a growl up from his belly.

"Fuck, man," he breathed. "Oh, yeah. Here, use this."

He tossed me a bottle of lube, and I squirted some on my fingers as he went back to sucking my cock. I spread the slick lube around his asshole and slipped my index finger inside. It slid in deep and John let out a grunt. I opened my mouth and caught his swinging cock between my lips as I finger-fucked him good and deep. He spread his knees wider apart, lowering his hips to allow me deeper access to his asshole.

By the time I had three fingers up his ass, John raised his head and said, "Man, you're driving me crazy. I gotta sit on your dick."

"Okay," was all I could say.

I pulled my fingers out of his asshole, and he turned around, leaning down to kiss me hard. His lips were soft and swollen from his voracious cocksucking, and we made out for a few minutes as our cocks jousted together. Sitting up, he coated my stone-hard dick with lube and squatted above it, then slowly lowered himself on me. I closed my eyes and leaned my head back as the slick heat of his asshole engulfed my cock.

When he was fully impaled, John sat still for a moment. "Open your eyes," he said in a husky, lust-filled voice.

I did, and we stared at each other for a long moment. Little did I know it was to be the most intensely sexual moment of my life. We weren't fucking; there was no discernible movement of any kind going on. John simply sat with my cock sitting snug in his slick, hot ass. As his green eyes bored into my brown ones, he tightened and released his rectal muscles around me with surprising force, stroking my cock without moving his body an inch.

And then, with steadily quickening movements, he began to bounce. My dick pumped in and out of his hole with a slick sucking sound, and I started lifting my hips to meet him halfway. John used one hand to support himself on the mattress and grabbed his own cock with the other. He closed his eyes as he rode my dick, my thighs slapping against his asscheeks as I pushed deep inside him with each stroke.

"Oh, fuck me," he groaned. "Yeah, get that ass. Oh, fuck it deep. Yeah."

I ground my teeth as I plowed into him, my staying power

quickly eroding under the bucking of his hips. Just when I thought I was going to lose control I felt the hot splash of John's cum on my chest.

"Oh, yeah," I growled. "Shoot that fuckin' load on my chest. Yeah, fuck yeah."

I was drenched in sweat and cum. The rank smell of semen permeated the humid air of the truck's cab and pushed me over the edge. I grunted and thrust up hard, pushing deep into John as I blew my wad inside him. He clenched his ass muscles, draining the cum from my cock before collapsing over me. He lay on top of me for a while, both of us fighting to get our breath back. His cum smeared over both our torsos, mixing with our sweat and creating a fragile adhesive that kept us together.

"That was fucking amazing." John sighed and stuck his tongue in my ear.

I was so out of breath I could only nod.

After a time, John rolled off me and rooted around in the nets hanging from the roof of the cab. He produced a ziplock plastic bag filled with damp washcloths.

I let out a bark of laughter as he began to wipe himself clean. "Um, do this often?"

He gave me a cocky grin and I felt my dick twitch in response. "No," he replied. "I mostly use these to clean up when I jerk off. Sometimes I've been known to have a partner but not that often."

He wiped me clean with one of the washcloths, then handed over my shorts. We both got dressed, and I followed him up to the restrooms again where we rinsed out the washcloths and used them to clean up some more. As we were walking out we passed two men coming in, and I noticed them turn and give John long, lustful looks.

"Did you know them?" I asked.

John shrugged. "They all start to look the same after a while. I'm looking for something with more substance."

A jolt ran through me. Could this turn into something more than a friendly fuck on the way to California? My mind spun with the possibilities as I climbed back into the truck. John and I straightened the sheets and got ready for bed. That night I slept nude with my favorite customer from the diner, his arm over my chest and his breath soft in my ear.

The next afternoon John pulled into a truck stop that rented out private showers. I snuck into the shower with him, and he locked the door behind us. The bathroom, one of six, was spacious and moderately clean. It contained a sink sunk in a wide counter, a mirror with plugs for razors or hair dryers, and a tiled shower with a bench for drying off.

We stripped and then kissed for a long time, our tongues lazy and familiar. His hands moved up and down my body, tweaking my nipples, pulling on my cock, and cupping my ass. He broke our embrace and lifted me up, sitting me down on the counter at the sink and kneeling before me. He sucked my cock as he pulled my balls taut, his fingers flicking in and out of my asshole.

Pulling back, John examined me then looked up. "You should shave your balls."

"Yeah? How come?"

"Makes them more sensitive," he said. "You'll be able to feel my tongue and mouth more."

I nodded. "Okay."

We got in the shower, and I watched him use a disposable razor to shave his balls as he explained his technique. Then I took the razor to my own. He leaned against the shower wall, watching me shave and slowly stroking his dick. After I'd finished and turned toward the water to rinse the soap off, he got on his knees to take my nuts in his mouth. I nearly collapsed on top of him at the sensation. My balls hadn't been particularly hairy, but the newly smooth skin sent every touch and lick screaming through my body.

As John sucked my balls and the water pounded my back and shoulders, I stroked my dick. I let out a grunt just as I started to cum, and he rose up to take my cock in his mouth. I stood over him, gasping and twitching, while he sucked me dry. When he leaned back and looked up at me I saw flecks of my cum in his beard and watched, cock jerking, as his tongue poked out to lick them up.

He got to his feet and I fell to my knees before him, watching as his fist banged up and down along his cock. Soon his muscles tightened up and he leaned forward, pushing his cock down to me. I let the first shot hit me in the face, the hot thick splash of it making me hard once again. Opening my mouth, I took him in and swallowed the rest of his load. It tasted so good I wanted a second helping right away.

We showered and dried off together, touching and tugging on each other and snapping towels at bare skin. When we finally stepped out of the shower room, a couple of big grizzled truckers caught sight of us and grinned, nodding to John in approval.

The drive to California and back took us nine days. We had sex each morning when we woke up and each night before going to bed. On several days, we had sex in the afternoon during our stop for lunch. We were versatile, taking turns bottoming for each other in a variety of positions. John taught me a lot about using my abs and core muscles during sex to make the experience more exciting for my partner.

During our final night on the road, somewhere in Indiana, we shared a joint as we sat kissing and stroking each other. I had come to know his body well. I knew if I rubbed his nipples a certain way or stroked his thighs he would get hard fast.

With his tongue filling my mouth I rolled onto my back and pulled him on top of me. I wrapped my legs around his hips and locked my ankles. He pressed his cock against mine, rubbing them together as we made out.

One of his fingers soon found my hungry asshole, and I moaned encouragement as he slipped it inside me. He moved down my body, his tongue running along my torso and leaving behind a trail of fire. John started sucking my cock, one hand pulling my balls because he knew it turned me on, while with the other he continued finger-fucking me.

Soon his face was in the crack of my ass, his tongue spearing into my hole. He nibbled and sucked and licked my asshole as I groaned beneath him. Suddenly his mouth was gone, replaced by the wide, slick head of his cock. He pushed steadily into me, our eyes locked, the muscles in his arms standing out as he supported himself above me. The sensation of him entering me was amazing. He'd fucked me before but never like this. John took his time and made every inch of his cock feel like a yard.

As always, just seconds before he was completely inside me, I felt a moment of panic that I wouldn't be able to take all of him. Buried deep in my ass, he paused and leaned down to kiss me, his hot tongue invading my mouth as if in imitation of his cock.

Then he fucked me. He pulled back, back, back, withdrawing his dick completely before plunging it inside again. His thighs spanked my asscheeks as his cock battered my hole. I lay beneath him, grunting and sweating, precum dripping from my cock into the hair on my belly.

John grabbed my ankles and spread my legs wide as he pumped his hips and drove his cock deeper. He shifted position and came at me from an angle, his dick sliding and scraping against as yet untouched inner walls of my body. My prostate

pulsed and pumped, and soon I felt the eye-rolling rush of orgasm as my cock spurted its load across my chest without need
of my coaxing hand.

"Oh, fuck," John groaned at the sight of my cum. "Oh, that's
fuckin' hot. Oh, yeah. I'm gonna cum. Gonna fill your ass up."

He pushed deep into me, and I felt his hips pump as he emptied himself. He leaned down to kiss me, and I wrapped my
arms around him, clutching him to my sweaty body as my ass
clutched his cock.

After a few minutes we cleaned up in the usual way and
headed to the bathrooms to wash up more completely. We slept
soundly together, and the next day, after he dropped the trailer
off at the warehouse, he took me by my friends' apartment. I sat
for a long time in the cab, feeling the power of the idling diesel
engine, inhaling the aroma of John's scent mixed with the smell
of our sex.

Finally, John took my hand and said, "You should go in."

I made a decision then, one of the better ones in my life. I
turned to look at him and shook my head. "No. I want to spend
the summer with you."

He grinned. "You're sure?"

I nodded. "Yeah. If you don't mind."

He pulled me in and kissed me hard, his tongue rolling slowly
through my mouth. Breaking the embrace, he gave me a sexy
smile. "I was hoping you'd want to stay. Come on. Let's go back
to my place for the night."

I spent six months on the road with John, riding the wind-
ing Midwest roads I came to love more and more. A few times
John took a couple days off between runs and rented a car. We
drove around California, visiting the theme parks and spending
a day at the beach ogling the men. One time he dug a tent out of
the storage area in his truck, and we drove into the mountains,

setting up camp by a quiet lake and having sex beneath the waning moon.

At the end of December I called my parents to wish them a merry Christmas and the conversation took a turn. They threatened to cut off all money for college if I didn't go back to school. When I told John about the phone call he surprised me by agreeing with them.

"Education is more important," he said. "Believe me."

One gray afternoon, as a lazy snowfall fell around me, I stood brokenhearted on the curb and looked up into his eyes, the color of summer grass.

"Drive safe," I said.

"Study hard," he replied.

I watched his rig pull away, the sick feeling I wouldn't see him again filling my gut. I heard from him a few times, late-night phone calls that turned into jerk-off sessions, but we never got together again. To this day I think of him every time I shave my balls, and the memory of his big cock and sexy green eyes never fails to make my asshole twitch.

SEMI-MARRIED MAN

Cole Bledsoe

It was nearing two A.M., and I was driving my rig full of shoddy furniture down the 5 Freeway to Los Angeles. As I listened to Moe Bandy and Joe Stampley crooning the lyrics to that classic trucker song "Semi-Married Man," I thought about my wife Teesha and how we'd just separated. The tension between us had been thick for a while. She said she couldn't handle my being on the road all the time. I told her she knew what she was getting into when she married me five years ago. But the real deal-breaker came two weeks later when she caught me sucking off my best friend, Bobby, in her own bed. Yeah, I know it wasn't right. But my getting married in the first place wasn't right either. I do love tits and pussy, but I can barely live a week without a thick cock in my mouth or up my ass.

Just thinking about Bobby made me horny. One hand on the wheel, I unbuckled my belt and unzipped my jeans. I pulled out my stiffening dick and stroked myself, thinking of my best friend's fat sausage and fuzzy, plump balls. Bobby and I had messed around with each other for nearly fifteen years, ever since high school. A couple of times we'd even double-teamed a woman. Both times he fucked the girl from the front as I pushed my rock-hard shaft into her plump ass. Sure, it was fun, but it didn't compare to sticking it again and again to Bobby, the way he writhed and bucked and moaned into me. He knew my rhythm and I knew his. I knew every scar on his body, every line on his face.

But after Teesha had caught me slurping Bobby's cock, she ran and told his wife, Debby, and our afternoon delights were quickly put to an end. Debby told him she'd stay with him if he straightened up and flew right. He agreed. I don't blame him. I mean, he had two kids with her and all.

Still, that night in my rig I missed him something crazy, and I pumped my cock over and over until I creamed hard and long. After I was done, I quickly pulled out an old towel and wiped my spooge off the windshield.

Yeah, that felt pretty good, but I longed for something more than my own paw on my prick. I remembered there was a truck stop about twelve miles down the road. I'd never been there before, but who knew what I might find. I took a swig of my Pepsi and pressed my foot hard on the gas. A short while later I pulled into the lot and climbed out of my rig.

The place looked about the same as any other truck stop in any other town in any other state. I took off my wedding ring, shoved it in my pocket, and headed for the bathroom. If I was going to find someone to screw, it was the best place to start. On my way there, I stopped at the doorway of a small lounge area that had a TV blaring. A handful of truckers sat around watching highlights from the 1982 World Series on ESPN. I stood there awhile checking out the tight package and hard biceps on the Saint Louis Cardinals' Lonnie Smith.

There was a row of folding chairs and behind that two worn-out couches. Three hoary old truckers with greased-back hair and long sideburns sat in the front gnawing on French fries and shooting the shit. The room was thick with cigarette smoke. But behind them…oh, dag, behind them was the finest piece of ass I'd seen in a long time. Close-trimmed mustache and beard. Deep chocolate-brown skin. Black flannel shirt and tight-fitting Levi's. A hot black trucker like me was a rare find in these parts—or any parts, for that matter. The guy caught me staring at him then smiled like the cat that ate the mouse. He reached down and grabbed his pecker through his jeans and gave it a few hard tugs. Good thing Ye Old Truckers' Club had their backs to him. Damn if my cock didn't transform into a steel girder right then and there.

The guy stood and motioned for me to follow him. "I'm Jason," he said, leading me into a poorly lit storage room and closing the door behind us.

"Cole," I told him.

Jason didn't waste any time. Within seconds his mouth was on mine and his hand was under my long-sleeve T-shirt, traveling up and down my chest. His full lips felt cool against mine, and he tasted like peppermint and coffee. Right away I recognized his Jovan Musk. When he tweaked one of my nipples, I moaned in pleasure.

My hands quickly found his belt buckle and zipper and unleashed his ten-inch chocolate tool. I took the hard thing in my palm and fisted it, slowly at first, stroking up and down the shaft and over the head. I pressed his fat cock head between my fingers then relaxed my pressure and slid down to the base. Over and over I pumped his meat until he stopped me and pulled my T-shirt over my head. Then he descended upon my nipple with his luscious wet mouth, nipping and teasing me until I was delirious.

As I massaged his thick rod, I grabbed his furry balls with my other hand and squeezed. "Damn!" Jason groaned. "Damn, that feels good!" He bit my nipple, and I squealed a little. Then he put his hands behind me and grabbed both of my asscheeks. "Boy, you got a fine, tight ass," he said. "Let go of me. I want some of that plump rump right now."

After I released Jason's cock, he deftly unbuckled my jeans and pushed them to the concrete floor. "Turn around," he said. "Put your hands against the wall." I did as told, the concrete wall cool against my palms. I was still in my briefs and didn't know what would come next, but Lord I thought I'd shoot my load any second. I turned my head to see Jason on his knees. He spread my asscheeks as wide as possible, and through my underwear I felt his wet licker circle my quivering hole. This guy was teasing me real bad.

When it got to be too much, I told him so, and he helped me pull off my briefs. I spread my legs wider, and he buried himself in my ass, eating me out like I was a $4.95 truck-stop buffet. Again and again his wicked tongue lapped at my hole, ran around the perimeter, then dipped inside. His mustache and beard tickled my crack, driving me crazy. "Sweet Jesus," I told him. "You are one talented motherfucker."

"I'm just getting started," Jason laughed.

I looked over my shoulder again and saw him put two long fingers inside his mouth, wetting them good with his saliva. I braced myself for what was to come. His left hand steadied itself on my hip as he eased his fingers inside my spasming chute. He was slow and methodical, like an artist working on a prize painting. He slid those two fingers in and out of me, and then I felt a third. He rotated them slowly, then plunged deep inside. "Fuckin' A," I groaned. "Fuck, fuck, fuck..."

After a while, Jason eased his fingers out of me, and suddenly

I felt his warm stiff cock slide up and down my crack. "I got a rubber in my pocket," I told him. "In my jeans over there."

"Cool," he said, and I waited for his fat snake to slither inside me. "Hey, what's this? A wedding ring?" he said.

Oh, shit, I thought, hoping he didn't have much of a conscience. "Yeah, but we're separated," I told him. " 'Cuz she loves cock and so do I."

Jason laughed, and a few moments later I heard him tear open the package. *Phew,* I thought, not knowing how much longer I could stand it without Jason's meat inside me. I stood with my legs spread wide, my palms flat against the wall. Suddenly I felt his fat dong slide between my cheeks, the round head searching out my tight asshole. For a few moments he circled my hole, then he burrowed his juicy tube steak inside me. It'd been a few weeks since Teesha had caught me with Bobby, and I hadn't had a cock since then. I felt full and relaxed, at home with the world and myself, like I was back in my own skin again.

"Come on, baby," Jason said, as he poked me over and over. "Come on and let me fill you up. Let me fill you up good."

My hips bucked to meet his thrusts. Just then I felt him hit my sweet spot deep inside as his fingers dug into my shoulders. As he pumped that fat, long joystick of his for all it was worth, I grabbed my cock with my right hand and jacked myself to kingdom come.

"Fuck! Shit! Fuck!" I cried out, not caring if the entire trucking world heard me. I pulled my hand off my cock and spat on it, then palmed my rod back and forth while Jason pounded my hot, tight hole. My hard, wet prick was full to bursting as he pummeled my sugar spot high inside me again and again. He grabbed me by the hips and slid that thing back and forth, slow, then faster, then slow again. I felt his cock expand inside me, heard his fuzzy balls slap hard and quick against his thighs.

"I'm gonna cum, dude," he said. "I'm gonna cum inside your sweet ass."

"Harder, man, harder," I told him. "Faster." I braced the entire weight of my body with one hand against the concrete as I pulled on my meat.

"Your sweet ass is mine!" Jason sang out, and I felt my body turn inside out as a creamy wad shot out of my dick and splattered all over the wall. Just then I felt him pull out of me. I turned my head to see him take off the rubber and toss it to the floor. "Turn around and get on your knees," he said, then politely added, "Please."

Without pause, I did what he said. His deep-brown rod was inches from my face. He yanked on his cock and rubbed the precum-dripping head hard. Buckets and buckets of sizzling jizz blasted from his prick, covering my face and neck as he milked his thick tool. I couldn't remember the last time I'd had such a long, relaxing, piping-hot shower.

Jason and I pulled our clothes on, then found some paper towels to clean up with. I thought about leaving my cum on the wall as some kind of "I was here" note, but my mother had taught me manners and I mopped up my juices. When we were finished, we left the room and shut the door, no one the wiser.

"Hang on a sec," Jason said as we walked down a dingy hallway with bad fluorescent lighting. "I left my coat in the TV room." We ambled to the lounge but saw the door was now closed.

"The old-timers must have hit the road," I said, as Jason pulled the door open.

What I saw next will be embedded in my mind for eternity. Grandpa number one was siphoning every drop of nectar from grandpa number two's cock while grandpa number three had his grizzled head buried in grandpa number one's ass. They were going at it like out-of-control goats and didn't even notice Jason come in and grab his coat. Slowly he walked in reverse out of the room and shut the door behind him.

"Holy shit!" Jason yelped, his eyes wide as dinner plates.

Incredulous, I shook my head. "Fuck! I hope I'm that horny when I'm their age."

"Me too," he said, and laughed long and hard.

That was nearly a decade ago, and a lot has happened since then. Teesha and I got a divorce. And so did Bobby and Debby. But Bobby got remarried to some waitress two hours outside of town and moved in with her. Turned out Jason wasn't a trucker, after all. He was just getting some R&R during a business trip to San Diego. Fortunately, we both lived in Sacramento and hooked up whenever we could, which was practically every night I wasn't on the road. After a while, my trucking life proved to be too much for him, so I retired and helped him run his property-managing business. Now I have a new wedding ring, one Jason gave me when he asked me to be his husband. And I am. I'm happy to say I'm no longer a semi-married man.

OWNER-OPERATOR

Lane Logan

I wiped the sweat from my brow, secured the ball cap back on my head, and drifted through the gates of Northern Roads Trucking. I headed for the double-wide trailer that had an OFFICE sign stuck to its side. It was ninety-five degrees outside, just warming up, and this sun-baked trucking yard was the last place I wanted to be. But economic necessity and a checkered driving record drove me on.

I plodded up the wobbly wooden steps, grabbed the heated brass knob, and twisted and pulled. Nothing. I pulled harder. Still nothing. I yanked, and suddenly the door flew open and the knob slipped out of my hand. I tumbled ass-backward onto the hot asphalt. So much for making a good first impression.

"Help ya?" a leathery broad with an orange dye job barked at me as I ducked inside the office/oven. She looked like an unmade bed in a fleabag motel. She was parked behind a dented gray metal desk, a smoldering cigarette hanging limp as a soft-on from between her cracked lips.

I tried to shut the door, couldn't, then gave it up. "I'm looking for a job driving a rig," I told her.

"Uh-huh." She pulled the cigarette out of her pruned kisser with a pair of walnut-colored fingers and blew smoke in my face.

We glared at each other, her watery eyes only slightly more bloodshot than mine.

"Got some forms for me to fill out or something?" I finally asked, wiping my hands on my jeans.

She blew exhaust out of one side of her mouth then used the other to holler, "Hey, Crud! We takin' on any new drivers?"

Something creaked in the room behind the scarred receptionist and fake-wood paneling, and then a heavy tread shook the NRT corporate offices. A man filled the doorway, all six-foot-five, two-hundred-and-twenty rugged, rangy pounds of him. He had steel-gray hair; a lined, sun-browned face; and a pair of pale blue eyes. He looked like the roll-call sergeant from *Hill Street Blues*, except this guy's uniform was a denim shirt and a faded pair of blue jeans.

He looked me over, a frown on his thick lips. "Get in here," he said.

I followed him into his office, Miss Wonderful shooting me a cackle as I passed by, ash hanging off her cigarette like trunk off an elephant. The nameplate on the man's cluttered desk read: KARL CRUDLER, PRESIDENT.

He planted himself in a shiny black leather chair and gestured at me to park it in the lawn chair set up in front of his desk. He grunted, "Let's see your paperwork."

I handed him my license, driver's transcript, and one-page work record, and he briefly ran his eyes over them, then snarled, "Owner-operator for ten years, eh? What makes you suddenly wanna be an *employee*?" He spat out that last word.

"I don't," I replied frankly. "But I wrecked my truck a couple

of months back, and I don't have cash for a new one. And my
credit rating's lower than General Motors' right now. And my
driving record is a little bumpy. So...I came here."

Crud grimaced, then rubbed his mouth with a big, brown
hand, studying me. "Well, I'm the owner and operator of this
outfit...understand?"

I swallowed what little pride I had left and nodded.

"You know how to handle a big rig?"

"I've been driving for—"

"We'll see. I got twenty tractors and fifty trailers, a warehouse, garage, and thirty *employees*." There was that word
again. "I run on winter roads up north that ain't nothin' more
than frozen ruts on a lake, summer roads fulla more craters than
the moon. I stock the remotest reserves and dock at the crummi-
est tin-can terminals." He stared at me with his armor-piercing
blue eyes. "Think you can handle that?"

"I can handle anything," I boasted, sweat trickling down my
back—and front.

"Let's hit the road."

We left the stifling trailer and reassembled on the melting tar-
mac, in front of a rust-pitted tractor-trailer that looked like it'd
just rolled out of a museum. A pair of gleaming eyes watched us
from the shaded depths of the garage, and then Crud told me to
saddle up.

I watched him climb aboard the rig, his hard buttocks almost
bursting his threadbare jeans, and then I swung up into the
driver's seat. The tractor had all the amenities one would expect
in a company unit where the company operated out of a mobile
home, which is to say none. No air-cushioned ride, no air-con-
ditioning, no satellite TV or radio, no GPS tracking system, no
nothing. Just a well-worn steering wheel and gearshift, an air
horn, and a few instrument dials.

I fired it up, cranked into gear, and the rig leaped forward.

"Easy," Crud said, placing a restraining hand on my thigh—a big, warm hand. "You gotta coax performance outta this old unit."

I looked down at his hand and up at his face, wondering just which "old unit" he was talking about. A smile flashed across his full lips, and I felt my own motor start to run. I drove forward, Crud pointing the way.

I easily cleared the drivers' course laid out at the far end of the yard with nary a pylon spilled. Then Crud told me to haul it out into traffic, and I neatly maneuvered the bucking eighteen-wheeler down some busy city surface streets, before hitting the highway.

Three miles down the shimmering pavement, Crud told me to pull off onto a gravel road. The road bisected an endless field of sun-ripened wheat, and two miles down that dusty lane, he told me to pull over. He set his hand back down on my thigh, and this time he meant business.

"I like you, kid," he said.

The cloud of dust I'd kicked up blew on by, leaving everything hanging out in the open.

I swallowed, my throat clicking dry as the surrounding countryside. "I...like you too," I croaked, and I wasn't lying. Normally, I hooked up with men my own age, but I wasn't averse to a more experienced hand every now and then. Especially one with the seasoned good looks and stone-cold build of Karl Crudler.

He moved his hand higher up my leg, and my body fired hotter than the air swirling in through the open windows. Then his hand slid over my crotch, covering me up fully in that most sensitive of male places. I hardened with appreciation.

"You got the equipment for the job, all right," he said, rubbing the rigid outline of my cock.

He leaned over and kissed me, hard and hungry, and I kissed back. His heavy tongue swam into my mouth, rousing my own tongue to life. And as we slapped our tongues together, I felt him unbelt and unzip me, felt his bare, calloused palm on my bare, pulsating cock.

He gripped and stroked my straining hard-on, flooding my body with joy. "Yeah!" I groaned into his open mouth. I grabbed his head and ran my fingers over his bristly hair as we urgently kissed, as his deft, knowing hand swirled up and down my raging erection.

He tugged on my granite cock, pushing my head back so that he could kiss and lick my neck. I sat there and took it, loved it, rolled around in it, the big man having his way with me, my body and cock vibrating.

He unhanded my prick for a second in order to yank my T-shirt up over my head, then went back to stroking me, stoking me, his tongue slashing now at my swollen nipples. He sucked on first one hard, burnt-sugar nipple and then the other, then bit into them.

"I'm gonna come!" I bleated, my balls tightening, tingling in warning.

"No you ain't—not yet," Crud said. He encircled my throbbing meat at the base with his thick fingers and squeezed. He sucked on my nipples for a moment longer, before finally releasing me. "You take it up the ass, Lane?" he asked gruffly.

I opened my eyes and blinked away the sweat. I usually came out on top, but Crud was running this show. I nodded.

He wrangled his jeans and shorts down to his ankles, then sat back in his seat, heavy, veined cock standing up tall and true as the man himself. He reached under the seat, pulled out a small, traveling bottle of lube, and greased up his cock to shining slickness.

"Get your gearbox on over here, son," he rasped, stroking his glistening meat slow and sure.

I took a quick look around, but there wasn't a thing moving on that parched landscape but the waving sea of wheat, our rig an island paradise in the midst of that sun-drenched ocean of grain. I arched up and pushed down my pants and underwear, unlaced my boots, and kicked everything aside. Then I climbed over the gearshift knob and into Crud's cock-cushioned lap, my own prick bobbing like a diesel-tank dipstick.

I squatted on the seat in front of Crud and his massive fuck club, feet on either side of his muscled thighs. He slicked up my crack with the motion lotion, and I moaned at the touch of his raw fingers, kissing him square on the mouth when he slid a digit inside my ass to test out his lube job.

He pumped me with his finger, our tongues entwining again. Then he grabbed me by the waist and pulled me forward, over the top of his mushroomed cock head. He stared me in the eyes and steered his huge hood up against my tiny pucker. I pressed down with my ass.

"Fuck me!" I wailed, the man's bloated cap punching through my starfish and plunging inside me.

I sank down onto his long, hard cock, impaling myself. He was halfway embedded when he pulled the legs out from under me, splashing me down into his lap, his cock shooting up my chute. My head spun and my eyes watered, the wicked, stuffed-full feeling sending me sailing.

"Jeez, you're tight!" he groaned, grasping my cheeks and lifting me up, dropping me back down, fucking my ass.

I clung to Crud's neck and sloppily kissed him, frenched him, as he hoisted me up and down and pumped his hips, pumping my ass with his spike of a cock. His breath steamed into my face, the sweat running down his seamed, handsome one; my butt bouncing off his legs and balls, chute gripping his pistoning cock.

It felt like he was ripping me apart, splitting me in two, filling me to the point of bursting. It felt fan-fucking-tastic! I bit into his tongue and frantically sucked on it as he blasted my ass, my own cock whacking against his stomach.

"I can't hold 'er much longer!" he hollered, his rugged face contorted with brutal pleasure and the bruising exertion of our wicked lovemaking.

I grabbed on to my cock and wildly fisted, speeding up my savage butt-fucking by helping Crud with his heavy lifting. My cock was a numb slab of meat, my ass an electrified mass. I tugged on my prick in a frenzy, bouncing up and down. And just as Crud's mouth broke wide open and his body jerked and he rocketed cum up my ass, I came with a blazing intensity.

"Fuck, yeah!" I howled, riding my lover, jacking long, thick ropes of white-hot semen out of my pulsing cock and onto Crud's stomach and chest. I came for what seemed like forever, draining my balls, Crud shaking like a wheat stalk in a westerly as he filled my blistered bottom to overflowing.

The dried-out dame with the perpetual cigarette gave me a knowing glance as I gingerly climbed up the stairs and into the trailer to fill out some payroll forms. "Crud drove you pretty hard, huh?" she cracked, blowing her lungs out.

I handed her a tight smile, eased into a chair, and started writing. I didn't much like becoming an employee of anyone, but Crud was one boss I wouldn't mind riding my ass.

CONVOY

Jude Gray

Hell and gone from any semblance of civilization, I pulled my rig into a rest stop and shut her down. I was somewhere in the middle of Nebraska, headed for Idaho with a truck full of women's apparel for one of those big-box discount places. You know the kind: lots of fluorescent lights, zombified employees, and banners screaming, DRASTICALLY REDUCED! After weeks on the road without a day off or another man's hand on my cock, I was primed and ready.

I'd been on the road sixteen hours straight. My ass was tired and my cock rock solid. I don't know what it is about driving so long that always makes me horny: maybe the vibration from the engine or the feel of all those miles passing beneath me. I counted three other trucks in the lot and decided to head to the bathroom to find someone else looking for a quick fuck. If no one was around, I'd jerk off then bed down for the night.

In the men's room I grinned when I saw a light out over the stalls: classic setup for quick sex. Soft, urgent sounds came from the corner stall, and my dick throbbed with anticipation. I ambled to the end of the room and pulled open the stall door.

"Howdy boys," I said, fingers in my belt loops. "Got room for one more?"

Three of them were crammed inside the stall—all big, strapping truckers like me. One had shucked his clothes completely and wore only black Army boots. He was hairy and hung, his cock jutting from a thick black bush. He had a black beard and long black hair that fell loose around his shoulders.

"Fuck, yeah," Blackbeard growled. "Plenty of room."

Blackbeard's partners were in their late twenties, both blond with patches of matching hair on their chests. The one on his knees wore a steel cock ring, the polished surface throwing back the dim bathroom lighting. The other stood with his arm around Blackbeard and sported a leather cock ring with metal studs.

I nodded, then pulled off my flannel shirt to expose my broad hairy chest. "Who's first?"

Two steps took me into the stall, and I grabbed Leather by the back of the neck, pushing him to his knees and stuffing my cock down his throat. Blackbeard followed my lead, taking Steel's head in his hands and pushing his thick, hairy dick between the guy's swollen lips.

"Oh, yeah," Blackbeard moaned. We leaned in to kiss, our tongues wrestling, before he moved away again. "You're just what the fuckin' doctor ordered."

Leather worked his mouth and tongue around my cock, swallowing as much of my seven inches as he could manage. His cheeks bulged as I shoved my fat cock head into his mouth. I pushed my pants to the floor and stepped out of them so I could spread my legs and fuck his face. Leather got into it and reached up to grab my balls. He had a strong grip, and I groaned encouragement.

Blackbeard turned back to kiss me again. His dark beard tangled in my brown goatee as our mouths devoured each other. Steel worked Blackbeard's cock like he hadn't had a decent meal in weeks. As much as I was enjoying Leather, I wanted to try something new. I pulled out of his mouth, leaving him in midsuck, and turned to slap my spit-slick cock across Steel's cheek. The kid turned in a flash and gobbled me up. He held Blackbeard's dick in one hand, stroking it as he sucked me hard and fast.

Leather must have felt left out because suddenly someone was spreading my asscheeks apart. Seconds later a hot tongue pushed into my asshole, and I leaned forward slightly, my hairy belly pressing against the top of Steel's blond head as I moved to give Leather more room.

"Yeah, eat my fuckin' ass!" I grunted. "Get your tongue up in there. That's it."

Blackbeard spanked his cock across Steel's face, drawing the kid's attention back to him. Steel snapped his head around, slurping up Blackbeard's prick as he stroked my cock. I leaned over more, and Leather pushed his tongue deeper up my ass. I was eye level with Blackbeard's crotch, and he turned his hips to pop his cock out of Steel's mouth toward me. I opened wide and sucked him down. He was big, real big—nine inches at least—and I gagged a couple of times as he fucked my face. One of his big hairy hands cupped the back of my head, holding it steady while he pumped his dick between my lips.

Steel, meanwhile, ducked down to suck my prick. His hot mouth worked my rod fast and deep while Leather feasted on my asshole. I grunted around my mouthful of Blackbeard's summer sausage and reached out to give his furry balls a tug.

"That's it, man," Blackbeard moaned. "Pull 'em hard."

I took his balls in my fist and pulled hard. He let out a shout and pounded his cock faster into my face. I closed my eyes and held on to his balls for dear life—it was the only thing I could do.

Before my back could give out, I let Blackbeard's dick drop from my mouth and eased myself upright. Leather moved over to suck Blackbeard's cock while Steel continued to suck mine. I reached out and twisted Blackbeard's nipples through his thick chest hair. He returned the favor, and we stood pulling each other's nipples while the two young guys sucked our cocks.

Blackbeard grinned at me. "Hungry?"

I smiled back and nodded. "Famished."

He reached down and pulled Leather to his feet, then got down on his knees. Blackbeard opened up and took Leather's long, pink dick in his mouth as I pulled Steel to his feet and knelt before him. Steel's dick was the shortest among us, but thick as a beer can, and I had to stretch to get my lips around him. My nose bumped the smooth metal of his cock ring each time I leaned into him. His hands clasped my shoulders tight, his long lean fingers digging into my flesh.

Blackbeard hefted himself to his feet and rumbled, "Let's head outside," as he tugged absently on Leather's dick. "This stall's making me claustrophobic."

We gathered our clothes and threw on what we needed to look halfway decent, then all trooped out the door. The parking-lot lights shimmered on our four trucks, as out on the highway a lone car droned by, headlamps lighting up the asphalt.

Blackbeard led us to the rear of the building and into a copse. We trundled through the underbrush. Just when I was getting ready to call a halt to our wilderness adventure we came to a clearing. Soft grass grew in a rough circle, all of it tamped down where those before us had laid on it.

"Dude, this is cool," Steel said, and his teeth flashed white in the moonlight.

"Yeah." Blackbeard shrugged then dropped his pants. His cock sprang out to point at us. "Let's get to business."

We undressed and moved in as a group. Hands groped, mouths gaped, and cocks jousted with one another. The four of us stood kissing together for a long time, the moon dousing us in pale white light. Steel broke the embrace first, leaning down to run his tongue along Leather's body. He paused to nip and suck Leather's nipples, one of which I noticed was pierced when the moonlight flashed off the ring. Once Steel slid lower down Leather's body, I slipped a finger through the nipple ring and gave a couple of good pulls. Leather moaned and pushed his tongue into my mouth.

Blackbeard got on his knees so he and Steel could work Leather's cock together. He pressed his lips around one side of the shaft while Steel did the same on the other. Leather pumped his hips, his dick sliding back and forth in their mouths. He moved slowly at first but quickly picked up speed until he was all-out fucking their pursed lips.

"Oh, God," he gasped. "That feels so fucking good."

I decided to return the favor he'd done for me, and moved around to kneel behind him. The grass was soft and cool on my bare knees as I parted Leather's hairy asscheeks and leaned in to give his hole a long, deep kiss. His hips continued to thrust as he fucked the truckers' mouths and I bobbed my head in time to rim his ass good.

Steel's head suddenly appeared on the ground between Leather's booted feet, and he reached out to spread my knees apart. Once my legs were wide enough he shimmied along the grass until my balls fell right into his mouth. He sucked and licked my nuts as he reached up to stroke my cock.

Moving my knees forward a bit, I sat my hairy ass right on his face. Steel eagerly lapped at my twitching asshole, shoving in his tongue and licking around the sensitive wrinkled perimeter as I did the same to Leather.

Blackbeard stopped sucking Leather's dick and went down on Steel. He was on all fours above him, his head pumping up and down in a blur of motion. Leather stood bent at the waist, one hand supporting himself on Blackbeard's back as Steel continued to eat my ass and I chowed down on Leather's tight, warm hole.

We shifted as if on cue. I lifted my ass off Steel's face, and Leather took a step away. He and I watched Blackbeard suck Steel's dick for a moment, then moved up and joined in. I lay on my side on the grass by Steel's head and stuffed my cock in his mouth. Turning, I took Leather's dick between my lips as he prodded Blackbeard onto his side and gulped down the hairy man's long, thick prick.

We lay in a circle slurping and sucking one another until Blackbeard broke ranks. He grabbed Steel's ankles and pushed the man's legs up into the cool night air. Spitting into Steel's asshole, Blackbeard edged his hips closer to press his cock against the man's tight pink threshold.

"Ready for it," Blackbeard said, more of a command than a question.

"Do it," Steel replied.

I got to my knees beside Steel's face and filled his mouth with my cock. Leather knelt on the other side, and Steel went back and forth between us as Blackbeard slowly penetrated him. It took a long time for Blackbeard to sink his entire length in Steel's ass. When Blackbeard's hips at last pressed tight against Steel's hairy, sweaty buttocks, Leather and I both moaned.

Blackbeard pulled back and drove in again. Steel's mouth fell open as if it were controlled by Blackbeard's dick. While Blackbeard fucked the shit out of Steel, I got up and moved over to Leather.

He knew what was coming and stretched out on his back alongside Steel. I knelt between his raised legs and wrapped a hand around each ankle. I spat on my cock, then aimed it at his anus. Leather reached back to spread open his cheeks, and my dick bucked at the sight of the rosy swirl of his asshole. Damn, he looked tight. My meaty cock head met wonderful friction-generating resistance as I pushed past his sphincter and into his ass. Leather groaned and thrashed beneath me, but I held his ankles tight and drove steadily onward.

"Holy fuck, man," I murmured. "You've got one tight fucking ass."

"Yeah?" Blackbeard asked, and leaned over to see as he continued to fuck Steel.

When at last I knelt fully embedded inside Leather, the slick wet heat of his ass gripped my cock like a fist. I ran my tongue along the hairy length of his calf, then pulled my hips back and plunged forward again.

I fucked Leather hard and fast, my prick sinking deep as he moaned and tugged on his nipple ring. Raising my face to the star-spattered sky, I closed my eyes and rode his ass with animal abandon.

After a few sweat-drenched minutes of plowing Leather's rapidly loosening asshole, I looked down to where my cock pistoned in and out of his hole and then to my right at Blackbeard's prick pumping in and out of Steel's hole. An itch started then, way up high inside my own asshole. It was a twitchy, hungry itch, and I knew I'd never be able to scratch it myself. I needed to get fucked good and deep.

"Hey," I said to Blackbeard. He turned his sweaty face to look at me. "How about letting him up to have a go at me?"

Blackbeard grinned and immediately pulled out of Steel's ass. I got Leather up on his knees and knelt behind him, fucking him doggy-style as Steel poked his double-wide cock at my asshole. The broad, fleshy cap of his cock head spread the lips of my anus, and my eyes closed as my mouth dropped open. Damn, Steel was one thick fucker!

Steel eased himself forward until he had burrowed completely inside me. Blackbeard knelt behind him and drove his huge dick straight up Steel's chute. We paused, all of us taking a collective breath, my cock planted in Leather's nimble hole, Steel's jawbreaker of a dick stuffed up my backside, and Blackbeard entrenched in Steel's ass.

Blackbeard started us off, pumping into Steel so hard I felt the power of his driving hips as Steel's cock banged into me. We found our rhythm after a few minutes and moved like a well-greased engine, pistons pumping and friction building.

"Woo, yeah!" Blackbeard shouted. "We got us a regular convoy!"

Steel's cock gave me a good ride, but it wasn't quite long enough to hit my itchy spot, and I needed something with a deeper reach. Before anyone shot his load, I slowed my hips and pulled out of Leather.

"Let's change it up," I said, and turned to look right at Blackbeard. "Want to test-drive my ass?"

He didn't answer, just pulled me to my feet and moved me to the tree line. He pushed me forward so I was bent at the waist, then planted his boots between mine. I licked my lips as I stared at the trampled grass beneath me. Blackbeard spat into his palm and pushed two blunt fingers in my hole. A moment later his fingers pulled out and were replaced by his enormous cock head. It spread my sphincter wide and plowed through the muscles widened by the girth of Steel's dick. Blackbeard pushed deep into me, then deeper still, his prick tunneling into my body with single-minded determination. I gasped and then shifted my hips, spreading my legs and bending over more as if straightening my torso would allow him to push farther inside me.

Just when I thought I'd have to call a halt to the archaeological dig he was conducting on my rectum, Blackbeard's hips pressed against my asscheeks. He stood, fully inside me, his hands gripping my hips and his cock hitting that magic twitchy-itchy spot high up inside my hole.

"Oh, fuck!" I groaned. "Oh, yeah! That's the spot!"

And then he fucked me. He rammed his long, thick hose deep with each thrust, and I felt my nuts pull up as his cock battered my prostate. I turned my head to find Steel standing bent over at the next tree, face turned to look at me as Leather pounded his ass.

"Oh, man," Blackbeard growled. "Oh, fuck! I'm close!" He let out a mix between a grunt and a snarl as his hips sped up. I held on to the tree for dear life, my hips swaying and bouncing like a rowboat in a hurricane. "Oh, I'm gonna fuckin' come!" Blackbeard said. "Oh, fuck yeah!"

One last powerful shove put him deeper inside me than anyone had ever gone. His hips throbbed and twitched against my asscheeks as he pumped his hot load into me. His beard whispered along my spine when he leaned down to kiss my back and ran his hands along my sides to my chest to twist my nipples. I stroked my cock, still bent at the waist with Blackbeard's pole stuck up my ass, and turned my head to watch Steel's face as Leather grunted through his own orgasm.

Steel and I came at the same time, our spunk splattering across the bark of the trees that supported us. We grinned at each other, then winced in tandem as our partners pulled out. I straightened up slowly, my back already protesting the position I'd maintained for so long.

"Thanks for the ride," Blackbeard said, and gave me a soft kiss.

"Thanks for driving," I told him.

We gathered our clothes and got dressed, each of us spent and moving slowly. As we hiked back along the trail, we passed two white-collar guys with expensive haircuts and hiking shoes. Their eyes were filled with nervous promise, and we stopped as a group to look at one another as the two newcomers continued past us to the clearing.

Blackbeard shrugged. "I got no place to be tonight other than back in my rig."

I nodded. "Sounds good to me."

The four of us started back toward the clearing, Blackbeard already unbuttoning his shirt.

THE LONG HAUL

Harlan Betts

For a long time I just drove. Put on some music, smoked another cigarette, kept those wheels rolling. Crossed the U.S. so many times I lost count, but I liked the long haul. Something about all those cities and towns, none more than a meal or night's rest to me, had its appeal. In time I had me a fine rig and made good money.

I had a wife and kids in Ohio, and distance worked there too. I'd married young but never much settled into it, which Lorene seemed to understand. She had the kids and a decent life; I had the road.

But years take a toll on people just like they do on an engine. The long haul—you could say that about life. So I was some years into it when I suffered what you could call a crash even though there was no noise to speak of, no broken bones or torn metal. What there *was* was impact, like I'd run into a wall full speed. Carnage without a mark. Death in some ways, pure accident.

It began at a truck stop, which is where I'd guess most trucker stories begin and I won't name the place because this is a confession of sorts. Middle America, though, more west than east. And it came on quiet, considering how hard I was hit. I just looked up from my eggs one morning and there he was coming out of the motel across the parking lot, shirtless, in jeans, tanned like he was in off the farm, blond, mussed. Young. He looked around, then reached down and adjusted himself and that caused me to stop breathing for a second while I considered he had probably just turned a trick in his room and was at that second freshly fucked. My dick was hard by the time I started breathing again.

Until then I'd never gotten up a man's ass or wanted to. A boy and I had wrestled around a lot in high school, and one time I came on his leg in a field behind his house. From then on we were always horsing around because it felt good being up against each other, though nothing was ever said about it. We'd be like that, playing around, all sweaty, and I'd come in my jeans. There was nothing more than that between us, though I see now there could have been. Now here it was again. It could have been the same boy, even though Bobby was dark and this one was blond. All that old stuff that had laid low for so long rose up right then.

The guy looked around like, *Who's next?* I had one hand on my coffee cup, the other in my lap prodding my dick, and I thought: all I had to do was go out to him, pay him, and go inside that room. I almost came with just the idea.

I never fooled around on the road. I drank more than I should have and jerked off every night and sometimes in the morning too, always with thoughts of a man going at it. I saw him put it in but didn't see where exactly. I saw his big dick, his ass as he pumped in and out or sometimes I just watched him jerk off. Lorene and I had sex when I was home, but that wasn't often. I was thirty-eight years old, and mostly I was looking at that faceless cock.

Nobody would know but me. Life could go on as always—only I knew it couldn't, that once I went over to him everything would change. There was something scary in that because I had a good life in place. But I thought of how Bobby had felt up against me, his hard cock rubbing mine through the jeans, and knew I wanted that again. Pure and simple. And there it was standing out front of the motel asking.

It was a long walk to the cash register. As I paid my check it felt like somebody was watching me, had spotted my hard dick, and knew what I was planning to do with it. My hand was shaking when I stuffed my wallet into my pocket, and my balls felt ready to burst. The motel wasn't fifty yards away, but it felt like a hundred.

When the kid saw me he ran a hand up to his tit.

"How much?" I asked.

"Twenty."

"Deal."

We went inside, and the place reeked of sex, which helped in a way. He pulled off his jeans as soon as he shut the door, and I saw his cock was a little pink thing in a patch of blond hair. He started playing with it, grinning at me. There it was, I thought. Like going to the edge of a cliff that's been there all along, only now you suddenly want to jump off. I saw myself falling, dick spewing cum all the way down. I started to undress.

Why the hell I thought of Lorene I'll never know, but she came to mind as I pulled off my boots. Probably because I did that at home, sitting in a chair in the bedroom, her at her vanity table fussing with her creams. She'd have on a cotton nightie and I'd get in under it and do her because that's what a man does. I will not share what I thought of as I fucked her, as she deserves some respect.

"I'm Jimmy," the guy said as I took off my jeans and underwear. When he saw my stiff dick, he kneeled and put a hand on it, which sent a jolt through me. I told him to get up because what I wanted was to get on the bed with him. He shrugged and did as told.

I stretched out and pulled him to me, wrapping my arms around him. I then began to wrestle a bit, feeling my dick against his, and it was Bobby all over again, only now we were naked as maybe we should have been then. We rolled around, rubbing, and I would have come doing this, so I stopped.

Jimmy got out rubbers and lubes and all sorts of shit, then lay down again on his side. His cock was limp, probably because he'd already come with the other guy, but I didn't care. I did, however, want to suck it, so I got down between his legs and put my mouth on him.

I fed like a starving baby at its mama's tit, and the little thing got hard in my mouth, which caused me to pull off and play with it a bit, something I'd done only with myself before. Even Bobby and I had never showed each other our dicks or touched each other there. It was all with clothes on, all just wrestling, but now here was a dick to have. I pulled on it, rubbed him, played with his dribble, and he told me I could make him come if I stuck a finger up his butt. I didn't do that right away. I just sucked his dick a while longer because it felt so damned good. "C'mon, make me come," he said and then drew my hand to his backside. "Wet a finger, put it in."

This was the line—or the cliff. I was on the edge, ready to jump, but I was already in bed with a guy, so what the hell. I wet my finger and ran it up his crack until I found his hole and pushed in. He clamped his muscle onto my finger, which sent another jolt through me. I told him what I needed was my dick up there, not my finger.

"Whatever," he said. "Just trying to give you your money's worth. Twenty includes a mouthful of cum."

I prodded him, and he squirmed and said to go ahead and suck him off, so I got my mouth on him again, worked his butt with my finger until he said to add a second, which I did. I could see myself doing it: a grown man lying naked on a bed, his finger up a young guy's ass, sucking cock and loving it. After not too much prodding he told me he was there, and I felt his spunk squirt into my throat. It made me suck like mad, like I could swallow his dick. It drove me crazy.

As soon as he was done I pulled off and rolled him over. I got a rubber on in record time, got some grease on him, then had his butt up and was in position behind him, cock aimed at his hole. Another picture of myself ready to break all the rules and who gives a good goddamned fuck. I saw now that I was the guy in my imagination. All my jerk-off sessions had been me going up an ass. I shoved in and set off on a hard ride because I couldn't *not* do it hard. I was so pent up, all that cum pooled in my balls, a lifetime's worth ready to shoot into Jimmy's butt.

Holding him at the hips I went in and out as rough as I could, not like with Lorene who hates it when I push too hard. I saw then how man sex is better because a man welcomes it rough, same as he gives it rough. My dick felt like steel, like I could fuck 'til I died, but then I felt the rise and I let out a string of filthy words as my juice began to spurt. Goddamn what a come—it felt like my balls churned up extra for him. I kept on and kept on, filling his ass and not wanting to stop even when I was empty because I wanted to keep my dick up him.

Then I was done and I pulled out, sat back on my haunches and thought, *What in fucking hell have I done?* But in the next second I thought of fucking him again, even though I couldn't—not yet—but it was like a flood rushing through a town, sweeping away the people and their rules or maybe an avalanche coming down the mountain to just bury it all. Either way, I came out on top, naked, dick out.

Jimmy rolled over and grinned. "Gotta hand it to you, that was some fuck."

I liked hearing this, even though I figured he said it to everyone who did him. "You get a lot of takers?" I asked as I dressed.

"Enough."

I paid him, and he stayed naked. When I was at the door he sat on the bed with his legs apart and I took a long look at the cock I'd sucked. "Maybe see you on the way back," I said.

"I'll be here."

All sorts of shit came to mind back on the highway—like feeling I wanted to put what happened behind me and at the same time bring it along. And this got me to thinking about the next stop and the next one after that, and would I now be looking for other Jimmys and sticking my dick in all over hell and gone?

That thinking won over any concern at the turn my life had taken, I suppose because a good fuck can overpower just about anything. That night there were plenty more truck stops along the highway, but none had any Jimmys, so I just had a meal and a night's sleep, then jerked off watching myself fuck.

The next night, one state over, I stopped at a bigger place, maybe twenty rigs lined up in the lot, and there were girls around, but I ignored them. I gassed up, got a meal, then saw a scruffy kid hanging around the crapper in back of the station. He looked like a punk, smoking a cigarette, and I didn't like his long hair, but my dick got hard so what the hell. I went over and when I went into the crapper I left the door open and he followed.

It was one of those two-stall piss holes and smelled to holy hell, but who cared. He locked the door behind him and started to rub his crotch.

"How much?" I asked him.

"Twenty."

I guessed that was the going rate. "Deal," I said.

He handed me a rubber, dropped his pants, then turned around and bent over. I just stared—for a couple reasons, I guess. One, if I did it this time it was a regular thing, which was both good and bad but mostly good. And two, I would have liked to wrestle him but saw that wasn't always going to be a part of things. I thought of trying to have him longer, maybe get him into the cab and drive out some deserted road, stop and have me a time. I ran a finger up his crack and found his hole, but when I started to play around he said to just fuck him, so I soaped my cock and stuck it in.

He grunted at this, and I was in a full-out, hard-ride fuck from the get-go, ramming my dick up him, which made my juice boil. No more than a minute later I was filling his ass with cum, looking down at my dick in him and letting go a load I'd carried since morning. I squeezed his buttcheeks as I emptied and wished I could keep my dick inside him, but it was over then, and I pulled out, his hole red and wet. I ran my finger over it, then pushed in and felt for my spunk. The kid clamped his muscle down onto my finger and pushed back at me, which I took to mean he liked the ass play. But I was done and knew it, so I paid him. As I got into my rig I wondered where I'd stop next.

This all happened three years ago, and since then I've fucked my way across the country and back, had my dick up more young guys than I can count, some more than once. I don't go home so much anymore, but I send Lorene money all the time, which keeps her happy. When I do stop home, I don't fuck her. That's the past and she doesn't seem to mind.

I would like to meet a young man and have him stay with me, ride along and fuck regular. I think about that as I drive, and it gets my dick hard, the idea of him there alongside, maybe naked. I'd like to look over and know I could stop anytime and suck him off, then flip him over and fuck him.

Maybe one day.

ROUGH ROAD

C B Potts

Some sounds are inherently sexy. The husky tones of a lover's voice, the sweaty slap of flesh on flesh, the rustle a denim shirt makes as it slips off wide shoulders.

But for me, none of that compares to the staccato rhythm of a Jake brake coming down fast and hard.

I hear that sound, and I know somebody's seen me. Seen me standing here on the side of the road, thumb out, clean-cut, looking barely legal.

Truth is I'm pushing thirty, pushing it hard. That's long enough to teach me how to work the little-boy charm to guarantee myself a good ride whenever I need one. And I need one fairly often.

Ninety percent of the guys who pick me up are pretty straightforward. Sure, I'll get the Good Samaritan types who try to save me, but mostly it's just a little suck, a little fuck, and they're on their way again.

But the other ten percent—that gifted, twisted ten percent—transform the whole thing into something better. They turn casual encounters into mind fucks. They play with my brain just as much as my body. Forget safe, sane, and consensual. We're talking something darker here, something sharp-edged and deadly.

I live for that ten percent.

"Where you headed, kid?" This one's big, six foot if he's an inch, tattooed down both arms. A tiny black-ink teardrop curls over his right cheekbone.

"West, mostly." I glance at his black pants, see the soft bulge begin to stir. Might as well feed him what he wants to hear. "Don't matter where I wind up, long as it's warm."

He smiles, hiding his teeth for now. That'll come later. For now, we dance.

I learn he's been married. Three kids back in Atlanta, one of them already growed enough to earn himself a stint inside.

"I tried to warn him. You try to tell your kids what they need to know, ya know? But they don't listen for shit." He shook his head and eyed me sideways. "How 'bout you? You listen to your old man?"

"Shit. I haven't talked to my dad in like ten years." An unexpected, inadvertent bit of truth—Pop wasn't in the market for a queer kid, and didn't mind telling you so—but it served me well.

"That sucks. You were what? Eight? Nine?"

I move my head a little. It could have been a nod, if you chose to see it that way. Which, of course, he did.

"Probably left you feeling pretty damn angry."

He changes lanes, easing into the slow lane behind a beat-up red pickup.

"I guess."

"Pissed off at your old man. How could he walk out on you?"

"I dunno." I feel my face get red, flushing at my imaginary abandonment. "He's just a bastard, I guess."

He downshifts into the rest station. The secluded, wooded rest station.

"And you? Does that make you a little bastard? Just a chip off the old block?" He's out of the cab before I blink twice, hauling me one-armed out after him. This is going to be fun. "You got any kids of your own, little sperm bags you made and left behind?"

"Fuck you," I snarl. I'm more than half-hard now. He sees it, he has to—why else the kick that sends me sprawling behind the rest-stop buildings? There's six feet of chain-link fencing stretched up in front of me, a Dumpster to my left. The only way out is straight ahead, through two-hundred-odd pounds of truck driver—and he doesn't look like he wants me going anywhere.

Which is just how I like it.

"Don't bullshit me, boy!" he growls. "I can see what you are."

"What's that?" I'd shit myself if one of them ever came back with the truth, pinpointing me as the ivory-tower academic I really am. Nobody has yet.

"Some spoiled-ass punk who thinks the world owes him a favor. Go out and enjoy yourself and too damn bad what you leave behind, ain't that right?"

Close but no cigar. My fists curl at my side. He smiles. I see the teeth now, just a glimmer, between the fleshy curves of his lips.

"Screw you. You got no reason to say that."

"Then why don't you stop me?"

I know an invitation when I hear one. I rush him low, hoping to hit his thigh with my shoulder. That might just be enough to knock the big man off balance, put him flat on his back.

No such luck. He sees me coming and grabs my shoulders with both hands. My feet leave the ground, and I'm staring into his big brown eyes.

"I don't think so, punk."

So I kick him—not in the balls, I'll want those later—but close enough to make him howl with rage. He throws me, a buck and a half of rag doll, hard down into the gravel. A big old boot follows, catching me just below the ribs.

I roll onto my stomach, scramble to my knees. My ass hangs invitingly in the air for half of a long second, and then I'm on my feet again.

A lucky punch catches him on the side of the temple. He buries a punch deep in my midriff.

Dazed, winded, we square off again. Left jab, right hook, uppercut. I block quite a few shots, but he's better than me, not to mention bigger. A roundhouse sends me sprawling again. This time he follows, pinning me to the ground.

"Best stay down this time, boy," he growls. Sweat drips off his forehead, stinging my eyes, salty in my mouth. "You don't want to know what happens if you get up."

And this is the moment it all comes down to. Can I switch homicidal to hormonal? I think I've read him right, but you never really know until you try.

"But I'm up already," I tell him, grinding my crotch into the rounded plain of his stomach. "So what's gonna happen?"

Half a heartbeat, and then the smile. This time there's teeth. "I'm gonna fuck your ass, you little faggot. That's what's gonna happen."

I surge up against his hands. Guys like this want you to fight it. True to form, his smile gets even brighter.

"That's why they say hitchhiking is so dangerous, kid. You should listen." One beefy paw drops to my crotch and yanks the fly open. I didn't bother with briefs—after all, I knew what I was looking for—but the trucker's a little surprised when my shaft springs out at him.

"Shit, would you look at that?" He grabs my hair with one hand while opening his own fly with the other. "You must really be a faggot. Real man would be shitting himself by now."

"Or I'm just not scared of you," I reply. I have one eye fixed on the eggplant-size bulge trapped in his briefs, forcing any fear from my mind in favor of sheer, unadulterated lust. "Maybe that's it."

He grimaces. It's not a pleasant smile. In for an inch, in for a mile, I figure, and continue. "Of course, if you're into shit games I'm sure we could figure something out..."

Thick fingers tighten in my hair, pulling the strands half an inch longer. "Let's put that filthy mouth of yours to some kind of use," he says, maneuvering forward until he's sitting on my chest. "Unless you want me to stick this in you dry."

Rough is one thing, violent tearing another, so I open wide. He has a big cock, at least as far as I can tell from this angle. The flattened tip of his cock head is nearly as wide as a closed fist, bulbous and already leaking precum.

Figuring this is no time for finesse, I gobble down as much as I can, slobbering as much saliva as possible over his bumpy shaft.

"Now that feels good," he groans, shoving more of his meat into my mouth. I half-gag when he hits the back of my throat, only to have his grip tighten in my hair. "You do realize if you bite me I'm gonna kill you."

Now, I've been lied to quite a few times in my life, but it strikes me that this is not one of those times. Making sure to keep my teeth tucked and his cock well out of harm's way, I concentrate on bathing it as far down as I can manage. My lips are aching, the sort of super-stretched feeling I dream about on lonely nights. The sweaty scent of him—half-acrid, half-earthy—fills my nose, while the black thicket of curls at his base tickles my chin.

The entire world has disappeared, until there's only this big thick prick in my mouth and the demanding pressure from the clenched fist atop my head. Far off in the distance, I hear the trucker groaning but don't pay him any mind until he pulls me gasping off his shaft.

"I said I didn't want to bust a nut in your mouth, boy!" More agile than I'd have thought possible, he clambers off my chest, yanking my jeans more than halfway down in the process. I'm jackknifed, brought eye to eye with my own sneakers.

Big hands on my hips, hands callused from hauling boxes and clinging to a steering wheel sixteen hours at a go. The gravel bites into my shoulders as he brings me up to him, angling toward desire.

"Now, this is gonna hurt you more than it's gonna hurt me," he sneers. One shove and he's buried head-deep in me, forcing my sphincter to balloon open.

"Ugghh…" I croak out just before his next stroke.

Now half a foot of his shaft is inside me, filling me completely. My hands scramble in the gravel, seeking out leverage.

The trucker smiles. "Don't you worry 'bout that, boy." One arm slides under my torso, lifting me half an inch higher. "Daddy's almost home."

One hand, gritty and covered with road dust, jams itself into my mouth to help me stifle my yelping cries. Inch by inch he feeds the rest of his shaft into me, slowly drilling his way toward my core.

"Look at you," he grunts. "Getting screwed in the dirt like a whore. Is that what you want, boy? Is it? Is it?" Each question is punctuated by another pounding stroke.

"God, yes," I choke out. My ass muscles convulse around him, twitching madly as my load starts to build. "I want you to fuck me, Daddy!"

That does it for him. His eyes close as a warm flood explodes into my ass, the grip on my hips growing incredibly tighter.

And that does it for me. Untouched, let loose, my cock is spraying thick white gobs of juice onto my stomach.

He stares at me a long moment, slowly backing off the way one does upon finding a dangerous snake. I lie here and watch as he arranges himself, zipping that behemoth prick back into his black jeans. He turns on one booted heel and starts to walk away.

Three steps out, he stops and reaches for his wallet. "Hey, kid," he says, not looking at me. A fifty flutters to the ground. "Call yourself a cab and get a ride home. Life's got more for you than this."

I wait until he's gone from sight before scrambling to my feet. The fifty slides in nicely beside its twin in my wallet. I smile at the sight, then pull out my cell phone. The guy was right about one thing: it's time to go home.

BIG RIG

Lee Stanton

It happened during the winter after I'd graduated from high school. I was a fresh-faced eighteen-year-old who had just broken up with his girlfriend, and my stepfather, Calvin, decided it was a good idea for me to take some time off and go on the road with him in his semi. The trip turned into a coming-of-age journey, and so much more.

We were held over at a truck stop in Dallas because of a bad turbo in the truck. I was slightly annoyed because we'd met one disastrous delay after another during our long month on the road. To say I wanted to get back to my friends is a huge understatement.

I was playing a video game in the arcade when I felt someone behind me. I was used to bored truckers watching me play, so I thought nothing of it. The game went on for a while, and whoever it was continued to watch me. I remember feeling a warm breath against my neck as the trucker put a couple of quarters on the dash of the machine.

"Keep it up. You're doing great," came a voice from behind.
I thanked him and continued to take aim at the monsters on the
screen. He drew in close, his crotch against my ass as he pointed
out incoming creatures. Suddenly I felt the cool metal of his belt
buckle against my back. The warmth of his breath against my
neck sent a chill down my spine. His hips ground slightly into
me as the feeling of his rapidly growing cock against my ass
made my cock swell against the tight denim of my jeans.

After I spent my last quarter, I turned to finally take in
the man who'd been turning me on so much. He was slightly
shorter than my six-foot-seven frame and had a full black beard.
His hair was black and long. I smiled as I looked him over,
reaching into my pocket and pulling out a cigarette from my
battered pack. He looked so much bigger and more powerful
than me. Though tall, I was a rail-thin one hundred and seventy
pounds.

"Need a light?" he asked, his face inches from mine. I loved
the sound of his voice, so deep and sexy. It was all I could do
to nod yes. "We have to go to my truck to get it," he said, not
moving away from me. I swear I could feel the heat from his
cock against my leg.

"Okay," I told him, finally finding my voice. After checking
on my stepfather, who was asleep in the TV lounge, we went
out to his truck.

When we got inside the cab he reached for the dashboard,
then tossed me a brass Zippo lighter. "There you go," he said
from the passenger seat. I lit my cigarette and made some
small talk about living in Minnesota. I saw he was mentally
unwrapping me like a much-desired Christmas present, but I
had no idea how to act on it.

"I bet you break all the girls' hearts," he said during a slow
spot in the conversation.

"Actually, I'm on the road for the opposite reason. I just had a rough breakup with a longtime girlfriend, and I guess I was too bitchy to keep around the house. So my mom sent me out with my stepdad, Calvin."

"You know what always cheers me up?" He moved in real close to me.

"What?" I said, my heart pounding.

"Good old-fashioned fucking," he said finally, his husky voice taking on a no-nonsense tone.

"Well, I haven't got anyone to—"

"Who says?" He cut me off and moved in closer. "I'll tell you something, I'd do you in a heartbeat." I've never had words take my breath away, but that time damn near did it.

"I've never been with a—"

"I'll take it easy on you, kid," he said with a smile. "If you don't believe me, step back into my office and find out."

I took a final drag off my cigarette and crushed it out in the ashtray. My cock knew what I wanted to do before I did. It was alive in my pants, straining to get out. My mind fluttered with "What if...?" and "How is this possible?" as I felt my face flush.

There wasn't much of a pause before I nodded and he pulled back the curtain to his sleeper. I slipped back and was leaning on the bed for a moment, trying to look around, when he came up behind me and grabbed my cock through my jeans.

I let out a gasp of surprise as his big hands covered my cock. He stroked it through the denim while pressing his hips against my ass, grinding much harder than he had in the arcade. The feeling of his big arms engulfing me overwhelmed me, and I melted in his grasp.

With record speed he had my jeans unbuttoned, and my rock-hard cock sprung out of my pants. He let out an appreciative grunt against my neck. When I felt him tug my pants down around my hips, I tried to reach behind my back to unfasten his belt, but he was too quick. Suddenly I felt his massive cock against the crack of my ass, and I gasped as I rocked my hips. He ran his hands down my smooth chest and into the nest of pubic hair surrounding my cock. My heart beat hard and fast as he slid his cock up and down my ass crack. I gasped as the head pushed slightly against my virgin ass. The pressure of his throbbing cock against the tight muscular ring of my asshole produced an intense feeling of pleasure I hadn't expected.

"Not yet," he whispered, as he guided me down to the bed. I looked up at him as he took off his shirt. Thick curly black hair covered his massive chest. His cock was thick and much larger than mine, and for a moment I wondered if I'd be able to take it all. It waved back and forth as he slipped onto the bed and scooted up to my face.

I knew what he wanted, and I wanted nothing more than to do it. I sat up slightly and let his big cock touch my lips. I hesitated for a moment as his thick manly scent filled my nostrils. Then slowly I let my lips slide over the head of his cock. The taste filled my mouth and my mind. I took his cock deeper into my mouth and sucked hard. I slipped my tongue around the smooth underside of his throbbing tool, feeling the warmth of another man in my mouth for the first time.

He looked down at me, his eyes closing and opening as he let out a long breath. I bobbed my head back and forth slowly then gradually picked up speed. My cock throbbed between my legs, but I knew I wouldn't last if I touched it. Instead I used a hand to work his cock, stroking it slowly while I rolled his balls around with my other hand.

The trucker rocked his hips to meet my mouth. I was forced to move my hand as he went deeper into my mouth. I wrapped both hands around his legs, and his balls slapped softly against my chin. His moans grew louder as he took over my mouth. Soon he was lodged deep in my throat, and I felt his cock press against my tight walls. I saw the desire in his eyes as he looked down at me. My brown eyes watered from taking him so deep, but for some reason I loved the feeling.

He slowly pulled his cock out of my mouth, and I let out a little groan of disappointment as the aftertaste of his hot cock stayed with me.

"On your back," he muttered, his deep voice choked with lust. I lay on my back as he pushed my long legs into the air. I watched his cock as it bobbed when he moved. A shimmering coat of sweat covered his entire muscular body. He dug around in an overhead compartment for a moment before pulling out a small tube of K-Y Jelly and a box of condoms. He tossed me a condom, then slipped back onto the bed and placed his cock back in my mouth. I sucked the head softly while I fought to open the wrapper.

His large fingers pressed against my asshole, and I gasped as I felt his first lubed finger open my tight hole. He pressed his big cock deeper into my mouth as he worked his finger inside me. My entire body was alive with sensations I'd never felt before, and my ass opened to take him in. The stretch hurt a bit, and I clenched down. I felt my ass suck in his big fingers as they opened me up.

"Just take it easy and relax," he coached me. "You're doing great." I nodded slightly, my mouth still working his meat. I had the condom open and ready, but the taste of his hot cock in my mouth was too much to let go of this early.

I felt a second finger work its way inside my tight ass. I tried to breathe around the trucker's pounding cock, but I could only moan as he filled my tight ass with his fingers. As the passion of the moment overtook me, I bucked my hips. He was pushing deep to loosen me up for his huge cock.

He worked his cock in my mouth, and I felt his swollen head pressing against the back of my throat. His balls slapped against my nose, filling me with his full scent. Soon he pulled his cock out of my mouth. I looked at it for a moment, shiny with my saliva. I couldn't believe I was doing this, but mostly I couldn't believe I hadn't done this before. I slipped the condom over his throbbing, slippery cock.

He moved quickly to my open thighs and lifted my hips in the air. I felt him position his shaft to enter me. As the tip of the head pushed into me, I gasped. I couldn't help clenching, pressing my legs against his sides. His massive rod slid into my ass, opening me wide. My toes curled as he plunged all the way in, his balls against my ass as he held his cock there for a minute. I wrapped my arms around him as he rocked against me. I reached between us, my cock throbbing. He nodded in approval as I stroked myself.

The hot trucker fucked me harder and faster, my moans growing louder as he took me. My ass massaged his every ridge, and I rode his cock hard, my hips trying to match his movements. As he grunted in my ear, jolts of lightning rode my spine with each thrust.

My body finally boiled over in a final jolt of pure pleasure as I shot a thick sticky load of cum between our bodies. I shuddered as my ass clenched even tighter around his cock. He hammered my flexing ass harder, his hips smacking against it sharply. My entire body shook as he invaded it.

He let out a deep moan as he came. He scooped me in his arms and pushed his cock all the way up my ass. As he filled me completely I went rigid in his embrace.

We got even with my ex-girlfriend a few more times before he had to get back on the road, but I never saw him again after that. Still, that hot weekend has stayed with me for the last ten years.

TRUCKER HEAT

Bearmuffin

You never know when you'll run into a hot piece of ass. Just an hour ago I blew a muscular, raunchy biker I spotted on the road. Yeah. Just sucked him off till he unloaded his nuts. I popped another woody just thinking about it. I unbuttoned my fly, pulled out my dick, and massaged it to a full, ripe hard-on.

Suddenly, I heard honking. I looked in the rearview mirror and saw an eighteen-wheeler flashing its lights three times, the time-honored signal that the driver was horny. My lucky day! So I pulled my car over, and he rolled to a stop behind me.

I strode up to the cab, my heart pounding with anticipation. Holy fuck! My jaw hit the ground. There he was sitting sideways with his brawny legs dangling over the edge of the seat. He massaged his wide chest and super abs, then dipped a hand behind his belt buckle. His monster cock strained against his fly.

The name tag on his blue uniform shirt said GRANT HARRIS.

The shirt was completely unbuttoned, affording me an exciting glimpse of his bronzed torso that rippled with corded muscle. His biceps bulged menacingly, their thick veins coiling under his golden-tanned skin like baby snakes.

Grant told me he was from Texas. I figured he was about six foot two and in his mid thirties. A raven ponytail cascaded down his back. Beard stubble peppered his jowls and a thick mustache curled over his full lips. His eyebrows joined over the bridge of his nose.

I licked my lips when he quickly popped his fly buttons. His thick, veiny cock popped through the pee-flap of his briefs, thrusting up over a pair of huge bull balls, like a rocket on a launching pad, ready to blast.

My mouth was watering for cock. Yeah, I wanted his dick so fuckin' bad, but I wanted to see him jack off, too. Much to my delight, he wrapped a fist around his cock and stroked it. I began whacking off too, all the while staring at his proud cock, which seemed to get bigger by the second.

Soon Grant had worked his cock to a frenzy, until the doorknob-size head was a feverish purple. For a moment he withdrew his hand from his cock, and I watched it bob. Thick precum drops oozed from the slit, dripping over his balls and coating them with salty sperm. I licked my lips and rubbed the head of my cock with a sweaty palm.

"Unngh, unngh, unngh," he grunted. "Here it comes, stud!"

"Shoot your load, good buddy."

"Wanna see my load, huh?"

"Yeah," I groaned. "Shoot your fuckin' spunk now!"

With that, Grant grabbed his monster choker, gave it a few hearty tugs, and out shot ribbons of cum that splashed all over my face.

My tongue snaked out of the corners of my mouth to lap

up the cum cascading down my face. Surprisingly, Grant's cock started to throb and heave again. Within minutes, it was stiff and ready for action. He hopped out of the cab and leaned against it, then husked throatily, "Think ya can handle it?" I just stood there for a moment, my mouth hanging open, his hot cum still dribbling down my lips.

I fell to my knees and slipped a paw over Grant's fat, vein-crisscrossed dick. I pulled back the three inches of raunchy foreskin dangling over the crown of his battering-ram cock. I slid the foreskin all the way back to his sweat-soaked pubes, exposing the wide cock that slowly oozed viscous salty drops of sputtering precum.

"Ya got one hell of a cock, good buddy!" I said. My drooling tongue shot through my slobbering lips. I hungrily ran my licker all over Grant's meat, lapping at drops of precum percolating from his spasming piss hole.

"Damn! Yeah, fucker. Suck my dick!" Grant howled like a mad dog in heat. He clapped his hands over my ears and guided my mouth over his pulsing meat. He mashed his sweaty groin into my face, forcing his dick all the way down my throat.

While I feasted on Grant's cock, I tugged down his jeans and briefs and inserted a finger between his sweaty cheeks. I rubbed my fingertip against his hot pucker, making him moan in ecstasy. Then I deftly worked a finger inside his hole. Grant cried out, "YYYYYYARRRRRRRRRGHHHH!" and his body jerked with erotic spasms.

As I continued to play with his ass, I drew the Texan's man-meat down my throat. Yeah! I was going to blow him but good. He squirmed more than ever when I plunged my churning finger deep inside his anal canal until I hit his prostate.

Grant went berserk. "AWWWWWW, FUCK!" he screamed. "Unnnngh, unnnngh, unnngh! I'm gonna shoot!" I continued to drool and suck on Grant's spasming cock while finger-fucking his stinking ass.

I clamped my burning lips over his thumping cock, and Grant hollered, "AWWWWWWW! FUUUUCK! YEEAAAH!" He rocked back and forth as his cock exploded inside my mouth. Huge hot wads sprayed from his gaping piss hole, flooding my throat with hot, sizzling man-jizz.

After he came, he pulled my jeans down over my hips. "Lemme eat your ass, stud," he said. He quickly dropped to his knees behind me, buffing his thick mustache against my ass crack. I felt his tongue dart into my anal cleft, my butt hairs swirling around his licker. Quickly I seized my cheeks and pulled them wide open.

Grant flattened his tongue and ran it along the full length of my butt crack with long, broad strokes. Soon my itching hole was drenched with his steaming spit. "Oh, yeah. Eat it," I moaned. "Eat it!"

He flicked his tongue tip over my puckers. I heard wet slapping sounds as he jacked his cock. His pants and groans were muffled inside my butt. "Awwwwww," I growled. "Eat my butt, ya fucker! Eat it!" I throttled my ass back and forth across his flitting tongue. Fuck! Grant was digging deep now, his anxious tongue plowing farther up my hole. He pointed his tongue and stabbed it right into my butthole.

"Fuck! Oh fuck!" I gasped deliriously. "Oh shit, fuck me, Grant!"

"You want my cock, ya fucker?" he growled.

"Yeah, stud!" I moaned. I wanted that trucker's cock up my ass in the worst way. "Fuuuuck me!" I screamed. "FUUCCKKK MEEEEEEEEEEEEE!!!!!"

As he placed the swollen head of his cock against my puckered bunghole he licked my neck. Then he bit my ears. He was chewing and biting my earlobes, driving me crazy. He ran his gnarly hands over my chest, his lusty fingers landing right on my thick nipples, then tweaking them.

"Unngh, unnngh," I grunted. Grant pushed forward with his hips, his blunt cock head pressing against my sphincter. At first my hole resisted. But he grunted hard, applied more pressure, and my hole snapped open. He was inside me, invading my asshole with his hot, turgid cock, as his fingertips twisted and yanked my sensitive nipples.

My body trembled as Grant pushed farther and harder up my ass. He had his cock halfway up my butt when I suddenly clamped my asshole shut, gripping it like a vise.

"Shit, fuckin' shit," I panted. Beads of sweat ran down my forehead into my eyes. I needed a breather before I could go on, but Grant was too fuckin' horny. He wouldn't wait.

"Hold on," I gasped.

"What's wrong, buddy? Can't you take it?"

"Awww jeez," I pleaded. "I need a minute, man. That's a fuckin' fat cock ya got there. Just gimme a minute. Okay?"

"Fuck you!" Grant yelled. "You're gonna take my stud cock up your ass like a man." He stretched my nips, making me cry in pleasure as he sunk his bull cock up to the balls.

"Yeeeeeeoowwwwwww!" I screamed, my body thrashing.

Grant pinned me against the truck. There was no escape now. "Pussy!" he growled. "Asshole! You're gettin' all fuckin' ten inches up your hole." He gyrated his hips as he worked his mighty cock in and out of my spasming hole.

He ass-fucked me with slow steady thrusts, then withdrew up to the fat knob of his cock head. My anal ring clutched hard around it, then he slam-dunked his meat into my ass, again driving it all the way down to his nuts.

He continued to finger my nipples, pinching and twisting

them hard at first then lightly flicking his fingernails against the very tips. I arched back against him, my pecs on fire. I screamed when he stretched out my nips and then sent them snapping back against my chest.

I felt Grant's pecs grinding on my back as his hot sweat dripped over me. His heart pounded as he power-drove his cock into my hole, digging the blunt cock head deep into my guts. He fucked me harder, and I gasped with each thrust into my hole. His potent man-stench wafted in the air, making me dizzy with lust. His huge balls slapped against mine. He had one hand twisting my left nipple and the other jacking my cock. It pulsed hard inside his whipping fist.

"Ya like that, stud?" he hissed at me.

Fuck! Was he kidding? My mind was awhirl as our cocks spasmed lustily. Incredible electric sparks shot all over my body. We worked up a funky stink as hot sweat poured down our bodies.

I pushed my ass back to meet Grant's pumping thrusts. "Yeah, fucker!" I hissed. "Harder! Shove your fuckin' cock all the way up my ass! Fuck the goddamn shit out of me!"

Grant rammed his sweaty groin against my butt. Big thick drops of precum gushed out of my spasming hole and mixed with my sweat. I grunted with each stroke of Grant's cock up my butt. Now he was fucking me as hard as he could. My head was bobbing up and down, my muscles flushed with sweat.

Grant squeezed my cock hard, making big precum drops ooze from the piss slit. I gasped and moaned as spunk bubbled and churned inside my balls. Just one more squeeze and I knew I'd shoot.

"I'm coming, stud," he panted.

His cock rammed in and out of my hot ass, ready to explode.

"Shoot your spunk," I moaned.

His cock jerked inside me. I knew he was ready to spooge.

"ARRGGGH!!!! FUUUCCKKKK!!!!!" he cried out. The trucker's cock suddenly swelled up, then exploded. I lunged back and felt his hot cum fill my ass. One, two, three, four, five jets engulfed my insides from head to toe. "Unngh, unnngh," he grunted lustily as cum continued to shoot from his cock. Fuck! He just wouldn't stop coming.

My cock expanded in the trucker's hand and burst with a thick, hot stream of jizz. Grant pumped my cock back and forth until his hand was soaked with gobs of creamy stud-semen. I sank to my knees, exhausted.

"Hate to eat and run," Grant said, pulling up his jeans and buttoning them. "But gotta go." He quickly hopped back into the eighteen-wheeler and rolled out onto the highway.

Shit! I didn't even get a chance to tell him what a hot fuck he was! But I grinned as I climbed back in my car and sped down the road. Sooner or later I knew I'd hook up with another horny stud on the road.

MOTION LOTION

Karl Taggart

When I think back on it now, it wasn't much of a plan, but at the time it was all I needed: hitchhike from Los Angeles to San Francisco to hook up with friends of friends who said I could crash at their place for the summer. Two days after high school graduation I filled up a duffel bag and caught a ride out of L.A. The driver took me to Bakersfield, which is where things got interesting.

The businessman I'd ridden with out of L.A. dropped me off at a truck stop, saying I had a better chance there as truckers were good about picking up riders, never mind company rules to the contrary. So I stood at the edge of a giant parking lot where rows of eighteen-wheelers made me think I might catch a lift with some guy headed to San Francisco.

Most drivers stepping out of their cabs went into the diner, and most coming out of the diner maybe had a smoke out front then got into their trucks and drove away. I noticed a young guy hanging around and after a while saw him talk to a trucker, then follow him to his rig. They both got in, but the thing never moved, and I realized what I'd heard about truckers was true: sex at truck stops was common. I thought about what was going on inside that cab—a blow job or maybe even a quick fuck—and decided what the hell, I'd follow their lead. So I wandered over and stood out front of the diner.

While I just wanted a ride north, I quickly realized that since sex was probably involved I didn't want to hook up with a creep, so I avoided eye contact with the paunchy, toothpick-chewing types, which was most of them. After a while I thought I might have to reconsider but then someone caught my eye.

He looked like he belonged on horseback rather than driving a truck: lean and hard, weathered but handsome. Marlboro man on wheels. He stopped when he saw me, lit a cigarette, then let his gaze sweep the parking lot and come back to rest on me. "You looking for a ride?" he asked.

"Yes, to San Francisco."

"I can get you to Oakland," he said. He didn't give me any special look, didn't check me out, and I thought maybe he just wanted company. I liked him instantly.

"Perfect." I picked up my duffel bag.

"Vince," he said as he started toward his rig.

"Karl," I replied, hurrying to match his long strides.

We climbed into the cab, and Vince settled into the driver's seat, then started the engine, which sent a rumble up through me. I tossed my duffel bag behind the seat, buckled up, and sat back to enjoy the ride. Minutes later Vince had crushed out his cigarette and was piloting the truck onto Interstate 5.

I didn't know whether to make conversation or not—he was that formidable—and I didn't want to annoy him, plus he didn't seem interested in me. Maybe he just liked to help out young guys hitting the road; maybe he had a kid somewhere he thought might be doing the same thing. So we rode along in silence, and I found myself enjoying the view from inside this beast on wheels. I looked down on cars, then looked ahead at the black stripe of highway that went on forever.

We'd been on the road about half an hour when Vince pulled out his dick. Nothing said, not even a look at me—he just kept one hand on the wheel while the other unzipped, reached in, and pulled out a good-size piece of meat. It wasn't hard, and when I just stared, he said, "Why don't you get over here and suck my cock?"

So that was it, I thought. They all wanted it one way or another. Some were just subtler in their approach, but hey, I liked sucking dick, having come out my senior year and discovered most of the varsity football team liked a good blow job. And this guy was totally hot. Just looking at him made my cock hard.

The seat was made for blow jobs: a long vinyl bench that allowed me to stretch out, get my head in his lap, and start in. I scooped the thing into my mouth and sucked, which made it start to stiffen and made him start to squirm. Then from out of nowhere he grabbed me by the hair and pulled me off. "Not yet," he said, and I sat up. "Take your pants off," he commanded.

"What?"

"You heard me. I want you naked below the waist. We've got a long way, and you're the entertainment. Now get 'em off."

I looked out at a landscape essentially devoid of life, nothing but desert scrub and the occasional cactus, and realized you could do what you wanted in one of these babies and nobody would know except maybe another trucker who might pull alongside. So I did what he asked, and soon my jeans, underwear, socks, and boots were on the cab floor. My hard cock stood bare.

"Jerk it," Vince said. He had both hands on the wheel now, and seemed happy just having his dick out. "C'mon, give me a show."

"I'm not going to last," I told him, and he laughed.

"You kids. Go ahead and come. You'll be ready to go again in five minutes."

I used my dribble juice to lube myself and began an easy stroke. Vince watched the road intermittently, his head turning toward me every couple seconds, lingering a tad too long, I thought. But then again he'd probably done this a thousand times and knew how to keep control. I eased down into the seat, spread my legs, and got a hand on my balls. "Yeah, I'd suck your dick if I didn't have to keep an eye on the road," he said as I pumped my cock. "You've got a good mouthful, and I do like the taste of come. I always get me a boy for these long runs. Get my dick sucked and then some."

As I worked myself I looked over at his cock, which was halfway along, and the idea of where it could go and how that would feel got the rise started in me, and I turned frantic. "Do it," Vince said. "Jerk that cock! Shoot me a load!"

I did as asked, spraying jizz and bucking up off the seat. I pumped and pumped, and as I finally emptied I saw Vince's eyes on me and wondered if he'd had them off the road the whole time I was coming. "Fuck, yeah," he said when I was done.

When I'd regained my breath I looked down to see gobs of spunk all over the floor. Vince just laughed. "There's Cokes in the cooler," he said.

I reached back, got a Coke, and offered him one like nothing out of the ordinary was going on. For a while we just watched the road and drank our Cokes.

I now enjoyed my nakedness. Miles sped past, the scenery never changing. Living on the coast you forget how much of

California is barren. Endless vistas of sand and creosote bushes, the occasional forsaken cow, but mostly that relentless highway. When I told Vince I had to pee he handed me a bottle, told me truckers don't stop for such things. After I'd gone, he did too. And we kept moving north.

By the time I'd had a second Coke, Vince was ready for more play. Without looking at me he said, "Show me your butthole." When I hesitated, he demanded, "Get your ass up and spread 'em!"

I tucked my legs up under myself and presented my ass. "Closer," he said, and I moved toward him. "Show me," he added. I reached around and pulled open my buttcheeks.

"What a pretty fuck hole," he growled. "Stick your finger in." I wet a finger and plugged my ass with it. "Work it. Give yourself a finger fuck." Again I did as told, prodding myself. "Two fingers," he said, and I added a digit. "God, yes. Fuck yourself. C'mon, ram it in, fuck it, harder, harder."

I did everything he said, but he grew impatient, told me to open the glove box and get out his big screwdriver. I took my fingers out of my butt and followed his instructions. The screwdriver was about a foot long with a yellow plastic handle. "Stick it up your butt," he said. "There's a tube of motion lotion in the glove box."

"Motion lotion?" I asked him.

"You know, lube."

Rummaging through the glove box, I found maps, assorted lubes, condoms, and a string of anal beads. "Just get the lube," Vince said when I kept looking at his sex stash. I greased up the screwdriver's handle, which was about the width of a small cock, then resumed my ass-up position and slowly pushed the thing up my butt. Vince then took over, and we sped along as he shoved the handle in and out.

"That's what you need," he said as he pushed the tool in deep. "Need a good goddamned fuck." I knew then where we were headed, and the idea of his big dick in me was such a turn-on that I reached under and pulled on my cock. I pictured that snake of his crawling up off his thigh and standing tall below the steering wheel. And I pictured myself sitting on it. "Fuck yeah," he said as he reamed my ass.

"I'm gonna come!" I yelled just before I shot my load all over the seat and God knows where else. I felt like an out-of-control cannon, dick firing wildly, to hell with aim. He shoved the screwdriver in deeper, which I swear made me unload a pint of cream.

When I was done I slumped, thinking he'd take out the screwdriver, but I was wrong. "Keep it up there," he growled. I heard him shift in his seat, knew he was working to get ready, and wondered if he wouldn't soon pull off the road and do it.

"I need more motion lotion," I told him, inwardly chuckling at his term for the stuff. He relented and allowed me to add more lube. As I did this I saw his hand on his hard cock and almost suggested we forget the screwdriver and just fuck, but he had a way about him that told me things had to proceed as planned. So I kept quiet, resumed my ass-up position, and stuck the handle back in. He immediately grabbed hold and pushed it in deep.

I don't know where we were when I felt the truck turn. After what seemed countless straight-line miles up the I-5, this was an event. We bumped along, and after a bit I heard gravel under us. Then we stopped, and the screwdriver came out of my butt.

"Get me a rubber and some grease," Vince said. He undid his jeans, easing up off the seat as he pulled them down, which gave me a good look at his thick black bush and fat balls. He pulled on the rubber, lubed himself up, then scooted over toward me.

He bent me over the seat, got behind, and put it in. "God-damned fuck," he said. "I'm gonna ream your ass 'til you can't fuckin' walk." Then he began to thrust.

He wasn't urgent. In spite of all the ass play, Vince was sur-prisingly calm and set up an easy stroke. His big cock went deep, and I savored the feel of hot flesh instead of cold plastic, not to mention him behind me and the smell of sweat and sex filling the truck's cab. "Goddamned fuck," he said over and over.

Vince withdrew once to add more lube, then resumed his stroke as if he planned to fuck away the day and had the stamina to do it. But finally, after what had to be the longest fuck of my life, he let out a low moan that told me a climax was near. He picked up speed, drilling me now, which got my dick up, al-though there was no way I could get a hand on it. I was pinned, impaled, and loving every second as he breathed hard, grunting with each stroke. I could almost feel his juice rising, and then it hit, his grunts turned to a roar, and everything in him unleashed as his cock spurted up my ass.

It was a long climax. He rode me hard, emptying those fat balls, getting off and then some, going on so long I thought he was maybe some kind of Superman. But gradually he slowed down, although his dick didn't immediately deflate. I enjoyed the feel of it inside me. Slower, slower, then out, and I quickly rolled over. "Good one," he said, tossing the condom to the floor. "Damned good."

He pulled up his jeans and got behind the wheel, which al-lowed me to resume my place. My cock was hard and I was ready to blow, but when I started to take hold he pushed my hand away, leaned over, and got his mouth on me. For a few glorious seconds this man had his head in my lap, my dick in his mouth, and the sight of him on me like that pushed me over the edge. I spurted and bucked like crazy while he sucked and

swallowed every drop. It wasn't much spunk, but who cares?—
it was him on me, and that was absolutely the best.

When he sat up he wiped his mouth with his sleeve, and that
gesture alone, the roughness of it, made me want to ask to stay
on with him. I was willing to live naked in his truck, have him
fuck me, suck me, do whatever he wanted with his screwdriver
or anything else he had in that glove box of his, but of course
I knew better. He started the engine and drove us back to the
I-5. Before long, civilization was upon us, then the turn toward
Oakland. Only then did I dress.

I rolled down the window and sucked in the Bay Area's
sea air as it crept back through suburban hills. Then we were
through the tunnel and into Oakland. At a corner near the truck
yards at the port Vince stopped and told me I had to get out.
"You can catch a bus to San Francisco a couple blocks up," he
said.

"Thanks for the ride," I told him. "For everything."

"You bet."

I hopped out of the cab, closed the door behind me, and
watched him drive away. As soon as he was out of sight, I pulled
his tube of motion lotion out of my pants pocket and smiled.

CORDUROY COAT

Shane Allison

There's no one in the park on this cold and foggy Saturday night, 'cept you parked along Martin Luther King Jr. Boulevard. Your arm hangs out of the window of your semi. The orange fire from your cig lights the night, and ashes are flicked onto the heads of parking meters. I park behind you in my mama's black Ford Taurus. I need to get out to stretch my legs after cruising around this park half the night, searching for men beating off in the azaleas, fornicating beneath veils of Spanish moss. Your smoke evaporates into the night air.

I get out, pulling my corduroy coat tight around me. I ask you how's it going, what you're into, and I feel like a boy looking up at you in your monster rig. I can barely make out your beard beneath these bright streetlights. You tell me you don't want to have sex outside—your ass bare naked on the cold cement picnic benches, my head buried between your blue-collar thighs like so many I've had before. You're a brown-skinned, muscle-bound, bear trucker with a thick head of nappy hair beneath a dirt-smudged John Deere cap. You tell me you have a room at the Days Inn. I'm a bit reluctant, 'cause I don't know who the hell you are. You could be a gay basher for all I know, out to kick some queer ass on the streets of Frenchtown. But I take a chance on you. You're too damn fine to pass up.

Your rig smells like good weed as we barrel and shake down Apalachee Parkway. You don't talk much. I think of your dick in those dirty jeans, twitching and hardening beneath the semi's steering wheel. You tell me you're married, that you've never been with a guy before but you've always wanted to try it. She doesn't have a clue about you, doesn't know you're on the downlow.

It takes forever to get to the hotel. I'm so horny, and you're a fine piece of ass. When we finally get there, you turn on the TV in the room facing Capital Circle. *The Golden Girls* is on. You excuse yourself to go to the bathroom while I peel off my green corduroy coat and striped knit shirt and toss them onto a chair next to the nightstand. I undo my belt buckle and sit on the edge of the bed to fumble with my underwear and loose-fit denim.

I smell of sweat, sliding stark naked beneath these cheap hotel covers waiting for you. I'm scared you're gonna come charging out with a knife, hungry to spill gay blood. I don't usually do this sort of thing, go home with the men I suck off in historic parks.

You come out wearing nothing but boxers. The Technicolor glow from the TV shimmers against your burly, half-naked body. Your dick hangs against your inner thigh. You keep looking out the window at the Saturday-night streetlights as if you're expecting someone to bust in on you in the nude with another dude. The cleaning lady maybe? The wife? You join me beneath the sheets.

We are two nigger queers naked as hell, our dicks stiff

between us. You fuss with your boxers, pulling them down around an ass of fur, past legs, ankles, and feet. As I fling back the covers, wanting to see all of you, our bodies together, our cocks throbbing in unison like hearts, you're startled. I take your dick in my hand and stroke its shaft, pull at the tender skin. I usually don't do uncut men, men with all that foreskin.

I try to kiss you, but you say, "I don't kiss."

Your milk-chocolate-brown sac is hot in my hand. I ask if I can suck your dick. I burrow my body into the sheets, sliding down the firm mattress, and take your love in my mouth. You smell sweetly of cheap drugstore cologne. I run my hands along your torso. A moderate amount of stomach hair forms a trail into an onyx patch of pubes. I always say, "A man ain't a man 'less he's got a li'l bit of body fur." Your meat is quite a mouthful. The head of it traipses against my tonsils, and I taste the hint of precum. The acute sound of a prick being blown fills the air. You push my head over your cock, begging me to deep-throat it, telling me to do the dirtiest things. I'm your cocksucking concubine.

Your fur tickles my lips as I listen to Bea Arthur insult Betty White. I slide my hands between your thighs to feel your hot ass. Your cheeks are smooth as butter, man. I stop sucking, leaving you wet and hard for later. I want to give your booty the attention it deserves.

I slide out of the bed. I tell you to get on your knees and stick your ass in the air. You refuse, telling me you don't get down like that. I assure you I'm not going to fuck you, I just want to taste you. I pull your legs, press your back until it arches, until your butt comes like a bull's-eye to my face. Your ass is off the chain. I bite into it. "Not so rough, man," you say.

I part you until your core is exposed. Just when I'm about to move in to wreak havoc, a car door slams and you jump from the bed.

"What's up?" I ask. "You expectin' somebody?"

You peek out between the hotel drapes. I watch naked over your shoulder as trucks like yours haul ass down a lonely street. I ask you who it is.

"Nobody," you tell me.

We smear ourselves back upon the bed. I want to start where we left off, but you prefer we just blow each other. With the sheets tousled and hanging from the edge of the queen-size mattress, you lie in the middle of the bed with your legs spread, dick at full salute.

I straddle both ends of you, taking your big, thick thing back into my whorish mouth as you take mine in yours. As I massage your sac, you push your ass lips into my face. Oh, how I love the aroma of a man's sweaty ass. We're in complete synchronicity as we devour each other's black dicks. When I suckle your head, you suckle mine. When you lick my nuts, I lick yours. When I finger-fuck you, I feel your rough finger slide up my butt. I reach around to push your hand away, but your fingers creep back to me.

With your cock in my ugly mug, I watch as slobber runs down your veined shaft, curving over your sac. You give head like you've done it since birth. I don't know about you, but I'm well on my way to busting my nut, and soon I'm gonna come all over your bearded face. I feel you fidget, your body tightening with every slurp, with every thrust my finger commits against your booty. When I tell you I'm close to coming, you jerk me off, paying extra attention to the sensitivity of the head. I suck you hard and fast. I grow relentless wanting to taste you. I can't hold back my load any longer and shoot off. I devour your dick as it tightens between my lips. You come like a geyser, filling me up. Your cum is slightly salty, but I swallow it anyway 'cause

I want a little of you inside me after our good-byes are said. I make sure I milk every drop from your hunk of love before I'm done.

I can hardly move with my limbs so sore. I climb off you with my dick soft and drained. I look to find your face and chest covered in my cum. You snatch three tissues from their flowered box and wipe my semen from your face and torso.

"Sorry," I say, wiping my cock dry with one of my socks.

"T'ain't your fault, man," you say with a grin.

I compliment you on how hot that was. I work my legs into my SpongeBob SquarePants boxers. You laugh when Rue Mc-Clanahan tells a joke in her Southern twang, and push your feet into dirty steel-toe boots. I button my shirt halfway and stuff my socks in my front pockets.

"Ready to go?" I ask.

You take another tissue from the flowered box and scribble something on it.

"This is the number to my cell phone. I have it on me at all times. The best time to call is at night. I usually make a few stops here in Tallahassee, so if you ever want to get up again..."

I tell you I live with my parents.

The park is dead, with only the hustlers strolling through the fog like zombies to keep us company. We shake hands good-night 'cause you don't kiss.

"Hit me up," you say.

On the drive home, I can't believe you were into me. As I pull into my parents' driveway, I realize I've left my coat in your rig. I dial the number you scribbled on the tissue, and you answer. The number's no fake. "Hey. Did I leave a green corduroy coat in your truck?"

"Yeah, but I tell ya what, I'll be in Tally next week. You can meet me in the park to pick it up."

"Cool," I tell him. "See ya next week."

I don't really care about the coat. It's too tight and a button is missing, but I figure it'll give me a reason to hook up and have a second go at you.

FREIGHT SHAKER

Rob Rosen

I was young, so sue me. I mean, really, the guy was sexy as hell: six-two, blond wavy hair, lean, ripped, and hung like the proverbial horse. And he was all over me like white on rice. Did I notice the bumps on his hands? Yes, I did. Did it stop me from tearing off his clothes and pouncing on that magnificent slab of meat like a half-starved lion? Hell, no. Would I do it again? In a heartbeat.

That being said, I did indeed need to work for a living. I didn't, of course, need the warts that spread from the top of his hand to the top of mine. Gross, bumpy, rough patches of skin aren't well received in the food service industry. In other words, I was a waiter who was quickly out of a job. I was also a waiter out of funds. The warts would go away, but my bills were there to stay.

"Ma," I said in desperation over the phone, soon after being fired. "I need some money."

"And this is news how?" she asked, clearly accustomed to such calls from yours truly.

I tried a different approach. "I have a medical issue and can't work."

"Try the free clinic and stay out of the bars." Her maternal instincts had clearly dissipated. Then again, she had five other sons, none of whom were the bundles of joy she had hoped for. Still, I was desperate.

"Sorry, Ma. I know this isn't the first time, but if I don't come up with five hundred dollars, I'm gonna be evicted. And you know what that means." It was an obvious threat.

She paused before responding. "I already turned your room into a gym for your father. The man's gained a hundred pounds this year alone. I swear, you men will be the death of me. Besides, I ain't the Bank of Friggin' America. You haven't even been home to see us in close to three years. What kind of son are you, anyway?"

She had a point. "A broke one," I said, honestly. I had a point, too.

"Okay, fine. Here's the deal. You can't work? You have no money? Come home and help us fix the roof, and I'll pay you the money you need."

Money versus Mom. It was a tough call. There were other reasons she hadn't seen handsome hide nor dyed-black hair of me in such a long time. She'd never been too keen on the whole gay thing, never fully accepted that grandchildren from me weren't in the cards. So we'd had a warm yet distant phone relationship since my coming out. I thought it was for the best. It kept things amicable.

Then again, broke was broke. "Sure, it'll be nice seeing you guys. It's been too long. I've missed you." You get more bees with honey.

"And we'll get the roof fixed faster with four hands instead of two chubby ones. See you when you get here." *Click.* My mom was more a vinegar person than a honey one.

And then there was problem number two to contend with: How was I supposed to get there? I had no money for a plane or train ticket, and, living in the city, I had no need for, nor could I afford, a car. It was 220 miles from New York to Boston. Thumbing it would be murder. I was speaking, I hoped, figuratively. I'd seen all those after-school specials and knew quite well the dangers of hitching.

I also knew the dangers of living on the streets of New York. The next day, I stowed my meager belongings at my friend Jack's place. Then I packed a duffel bag, put a few Band-Aids on my warted hand, and headed for the highway. Well, to be more precise, I headed for a rest stop I'd frequented before. Only this time I needed a ride, not a blow job.

Jack dropped me off.

"Wish me luck," I said as I hopped out of his car.

He looked me up and down, from my Daisy Dukes to my plunging tank top, and said, shaking his head, "If I don't hear from you in twenty-four hours, I'm calling the police."

It was nice to be loved, and looked out for. It would've been nicer still if he had offered me a ride all the way to Boston. In any case, at least I was at a good starting point and the parking lot was already full of cars and trucks, as it usually was that time of day. And though I'd never hitched before, I'd certainly had other forms of luck at this particular rest stop.

I looked around, found a nice stretch of lawn, sat on my duffel, and placed a sign—which I'd quickly scribbled before leaving—between my hairy, muscular thighs. BOSTON OR BUST, it read. Short but sweet.

Fortunately, I didn't have long to wait for a response.

"You headed to Boston?" the guy asked, on his way out of the restroom.

"So the sign says," I replied with a smile.

"Now, that's a coincidence. So am I." He stood with his arms akimbo and nodded toward the rear of the parking lot. "See that truck over there? I'm haulin' from Atlanta to Boston. Wouldn't mind some company, seein' as we're goin' to the same place and all."

I gave him the once-over. For a trucker, he wasn't half-bad looking. He was short, thick, and cute. His arms and biceps bulged with thick veins, stretching his tight, blue, button-down shirt to its limits. A fine tuft of black hair peeked out over the top button, and stitched on the shirt was HENRY in fine script. He wore matching blue slacks, which showed off his defined, squat legs. A fetching lump rested in the slacks' crotch area. I imagined what he was hiding in there. I almost groaned at the thought but caught myself.

Given the crow's-feet and the gray in his sideburns, I'd have guessed him to be in his late thirties. Still, he was handsome, even though he was old enough to be my father, just about. I liked the unshaven, strong jaw; the small, button nose; the thick full lips. Most of all, I liked his piercing blue eyes. Okay, most of all, I liked that he was headed to Boston. It was the icing on his thick, creamy cake. And the cherry on top was that my gaydar was going off at full force.

"Well," I said, offering him my hand, "since we're both going to Boston, why not?" He grabbed my smallish hand with his big, strong, calloused one and helped me up. "Name's Rob," I said, shaking his mitt.

"Henry," he said, pointing to his shirt. "Nice to meet you." He winked at me.

I nodded and followed him to his truck. I didn't know, and

still don't, all the nomenclature for the style and size of it. I couldn't tell you how many axles it had or the horsepower. But I will say this, it was one big truck. And though I was glad for the ride, I was a bit nervous.

It must've shown. "First time?" he asked. "In a truck, I mean?"

"First time in a truck. First time hitching a ride." I smiled uneasily at him as we both slammed our doors shut and put on our seat belts.

Everything inside the cab was new and different: the big bucket seats, the giant steering wheel, the gearshift, the front window, even the cab itself. Not to mention the altitude change. It was strange driving so high off the ground. It was also kind of erotic being able to stare down into everyone's lap.

A few miles down the road, I asked, "Bet you've seen a lot of weird things from up here, huh?"

Henry laughed. "Not too weird, no. Though some people seem to like to drive with their pants down and their privates out. Guess they like that it's taboo, or something like that."

I didn't comment right away, though the thought had already crossed my mind. Instead I focused on a photo he had taped up above the window. "That your wife and kids?" I asked.

He looked at the picture and smiled. "My sister and her kids. I ain't married. You?"

I giggled despite myself. "Um, no. Not married."

He looked over at me and asked, "Wanna be? I mean, some-day?" He blushed and quickly looked back at the road. "I didn't mean to me, I just meant in general, you know," he blurted. "Jeez, no wonder I never pick up hitchers. You must think I'm a nutjob, huh?"

"Actually," I said, "I think you're kind of cute, if you don't mind me saying." I knew I was probably pushing my luck, but I figured the worst he could do was kick me out.

Fortunately, he did no such thing. "Cute, huh? Been accused of lots of things before, but never that. You're cute yourself, Rob." Again he smiled in a gosh-golly kinda way that only added to his charm.

I thanked him and stared ahead. He cranked the radio up, and we drove in silence for a few dozen miles. I leaned my head back and shut my eyes, fantasizing about all the things I'd like to do with Henry besides ride shotgun.

Eventually I got my nerve up and said, "You know, getting back to seeing those people with their pants pulled down, I sort of see what all the excitement is about."

"Yeah?" He shot a quick glance my way.

"Well, yeah. I mean, it's kind of hot to have your privates out while all those strangers go zooming by and no one is the wiser except you. That is, you and any truckers that might pass by, right?"

"I suppose so. You ever done it?" I detected a slight tremor in his voice.

"Nope. I'm a city boy. I rarely get to drive in a car anymore."

"Well, this ain't a car, strictly speaking, and there's no one passing by that can look in here."

I got his drift in an instant. "Hmm," I said, pretending to think about it. "I could, I suppose, unbutton my shorts." Which I promptly did.

"Child's play," he said.

"Is that a dare?"

"Take it as you like." He laughed.

The zipper came down next. "And this?" I said.

He looked over and down. "Nice jockstrap," he commented. "Never seen one in red before."

"Christmas gift, see?" I said, pulling the shorts down even more to reveal a reindeer face covering my nut sac.

"You must've been a good boy." Again he laughed, and then tugged at his crotch for good measure. "Does the nose glow?"

"As a matter of fact," I said, pressing a button inside. "It does." A flashing red light illuminated the seat.

"Well now, what will they think of next?" He gave a hearty chuckle. It was contagious, and before long both of us were laughing hysterically.

"You should get yourself a pair," I said, when I'd at last caught my breath. "You'd look good in them. Better yet, you can have mine."

"Really?" he said as he watched me pull my shorty shorts down over my sneakers then kick them to the floor. The jock slid off next.

"Here," I said. "It's a bit late, but merry Christmas." I placed the jock on his lap. I could feel the bulge beneath his slacks, but he was driving a big-ass truck, so I knew better than to start messing with his clothes. That, of course, didn't stop me from continuing with my own shenanigans.

"Thank you, Rob. That was right nice of you."

"You're very welcome." I sat back in my seat, watching the cars and the landscape stream by. "You know something, Henry?" I said, after a time. "It is hot being almost naked with all these people driving by."

"I can see that," he said with a glance down at my expanding cock.

"Well, now, keep your eyes on the road. Wouldn't want to kill anyone, especially us."

And though I was mildly teasing him, what I said was true. It was hot to be almost naked. Way hot. But then I figured, why not all the way naked? My tank top joined the shorts a second later. Then I hopped up on the seat and put my back against the passenger window so that I was crouching and facing Henry. My cock bobbed as we hit the bumps along the highway.

Henry eyed me from top to bottom. I took my thumb and forefinger and worked my right nipple. My cock twitched, as did the driver.

"Hey, now. Two can play at this game." He took one of his hands off the steering wheel then deftly pulled his short, thick cock out of his slacks. Then he quickly put both hands back on the wheel. "Yep, that is exciting, just like you said."

"Say, Henry?" I said, as I continued tweaking my nipple. My other hand pulled down hard on my swaying nuts.

"Yes, Rob?"

"Could you drive with a pair of lips around that fat dick of yours?" I was going for broke.

"Only one way to find out. Besides, I am a really good driver."

"And I'm a really good blower." I sat back down and leaned over to his side of the cab. First I just held that big slab of meat in my hand, stroking it slowly and getting a feel for it. I slapped the huge mushroom head on my palm then pushed it down toward his lap so I could watch it spring back up.

"No accidents yet," he said, egging me on.

I leaned in farther and this time slapped his cock against my face. It made a nice thumping sound. I liked the smell of his hefty prick, too. Musty. Manly. Sweaty. That's the way it tasted too, when I finally slipped the massive head into my mouth; I got a dose of his sweet precum as I worked the thick cock farther in. The entire length fit nicely inside. It wasn't a long dick, but man it truly was wide. I gagged but kept going at it from top to bottom, alternating between sucking and licking and stroking it.

It was then I felt us turning off the highway, but since we

weren't careening off the side of the road or ramming into un-suspecting motorists, I decided to continue with the job at hand. I closed my eyes and wondered what the rest of him looked like. His balls. His ass. His legs and chest.

I didn't have long to wait.

The truck came to a stop a few minutes later. I released his fat dick and sat back up. We were at a truck stop, parked way in the back. "Hey, Rob," he said, when he had turned off the ignition.

"Yeah?" I said. "What can I do for ya?"

"Those lips good for anything else?" He leaned over and stared at me with those big, blue eyes. I leaned in too, and gently, softly, tenderly kissed his thick lips. He kissed me back, only rougher, with more urgency. Our tongues swirled and our lips pressed hard. His hand quickly found the nipple I'd been playing with. I moaned in appreciation.

"This thing got a bed?" I rasped in his ear before I sucked and bit on a tender earlobe.

"Better than that," he replied. He stepped between the seats and crouched behind them. There was a bed in the cab, but there was also a door. He unlatched it and pushed it open. "Come on," he said, grabbing my hand and leading me into the belly of the beast.

Naked and hard I entered the back of the truck. It was nearly full of crates, I saw, once Henry turned on an overhead light. "What's in these things?" I asked. "Engines? Blue jeans? Tools?"

"Nope," he said with a laugh as he reached over and cupped my balls. "Canned vegetables. Lots of 'em."

Now it was my turn to laugh. I'd pictured something more manly, obviously. "I suppose people need their veggies," I said.

"Yep," he said. "Suppose so."

That's when I remembered something. "Be right back," I hollered, and crawled back to the cab and retrieved my fancy jockstrap. "Here, try it on for size."

Henry smiled and laughed before taking it from my hand. I sat on a crate and readied myself for the show. Slowly, for my benefit I suppose, he undid one button on his shirt at a time. The tuft of hair I'd seen at the first rest stop trailed down and out, completely covering his chest and belly. The guy was in great shape. His torso was ripped with solid muscle. All that heavy lifting, I guessed. He dropped the shirt to the floor. My hand kept my boner going.

He bent down and untied his boots, then kicked them against a crate and continued with the show. The blue slacks were unbuttoned and fell to the floor to reveal matching blue boxers that tented in my direction. The rest of his clothes quickly followed. Henry stood naked in front of me, stroking his short, fat cock.

"Maybe we can skip the jockstrap for now," I said as I admired the trucker's hard body and equally hard dick.

"Good idea," he replied, and moved closer to me to continue with our kissing. His bristly facial hair tickled my chin and cheeks.

"Hey, Henry," I said, after a few minutes of this. "Can you hop up on this crate?" He did, and I hopped down. "Now, um, turn around and squat." He did this as well, so that I now had a nice view of his muscled, hairy ass, which hung slightly over the edge of the crate.

I spanked his rump, and the noise echoed throughout the back of the truck. Then I rubbed my hand over and around the breadth and width of it. His ass was wide but firm and covered in hair, especially the crack. I spread his cheeks apart for a better view of the pink center. It too was covered in curly, black fuzz.

"Tastes better than it looks," he said.

He was right, I quickly found out. I lapped at the hole with my tongue. It was musky, like the rest of him. I sucked on his asshole then probed it with my tongue. Henry seemed to enjoy the attention to his nether region. I reached between his legs and pulled his thick cock through his legs and to my lips. I alternated between sucking on that and his asshole. Then my index finger found its way inside, gliding in and out. Henry gasped but then relaxed and pushed his meaty ass farther down.

"Try two," he commanded.

I spit on his asshole, then did as he asked, all the while sucking on his cock and low-hanging, hairy balls. The two fingers fit comfortably, just like his cock in my mouth. When I felt his prostate harden beneath my fingers, I stopped.

"Not yet, Henry," I said.

He turned around and hopped down to join me, encasing me in his big arms as he sucked on my mouth and kneaded my asscheeks. "My turn," he finally said, then crouched to take my cock into his mouth. The guy was a pro, taking my full seven inches down to the base. My heavy nuts followed suit as he took each of them into his wet mouth. And then his fingers, like mine had with him, found their way to my hairless hole.

"Wait," I told him, then crouched as well.

"That'll work," he said as he again stroked my cock and, spitting on his fingers, teased my hole. I mimicked his actions with my own. All the while we kissed, stopping intermittently to look each other in the eyes. I couldn't get enough of those sparkling-blue peepers.

As he gingerly worked a finger in my hole, I did the same to his. When he worked the second one in, so did I, until both of us were double finger-fucking each other and stroking hard and fast on our cocks.

"Ready?" he groaned in my ear several minutes later.

"Uh-huh," I eagerly replied.

Then, with our fingers entrenched to the hilt, we both came in big, gooey globs of cum. Mine hit his stomach, his hit my thigh. Our moans filled the cavernous truck. When the last drops of cum had been coaxed out, we both giggled and gently removed our fingers.

"That was fun," I said, as I sat down on the cold metal floor.

"Yep," he said, joining me there.

Henry and I kissed some more, and eventually he got up to find us a towel. Then we got dressed, him in my reindeer jock and me in his boxers. He laughed when I reached over and pressed the button that caused the nose to blink. I laughed with him, and gave him a final, deep, soulful kiss before we continued on our journey to Boston.

Three hours later we were pulling up to my parents' house.

"Well, Henry, thanks again. For everything," I told him.

"My pleasure," he said.

"Both our pleasures," I added with a grin.

I leaned in and gave him a farewell kiss on his gloriously full lips. Our eyes locked one last time, then he whispered in my ear, "And thanks for the jock. I'll think of you every time I light up."

"Don't mention it," I said. "Because someday I just might."

And now, at last, I have.

G.T.C.

Terry Hopkins

It was 1977, and I was twenty-four years old. I'd just gotten kicked out of the Navy for being a faggot and didn't know what I was going to do next. That's when my buddy Mark suggested I enroll in trucking school with him. I'd heard plenty of tales of hot, gay sex on the road, and since I no longer had any bunkmates to screw, I figured being a trucker would be the next best thing.

Boy, was I right.

The first day of class, my gaydar was going off in all directions. In our group of about twenty students, I guessed that at least half were gay. I'd later be proven a statistical genius.

First there was the crew-cut, bearded hulk of a man sitting in the front row. He had tree-trunk arms and a massive chest that tapered down to a trim waist. He wore a red-plaid flannel shirt cut off at the shoulders, and a black cobra tattoo wrapped around his beefy, sweat-sheened biceps.

"Check out Mr. Meaty Meat," Mark whispered to me. "Fuckin' A. I'd like to give him a big ol' lick in all the right places."

"Not to mention B.B. over there."

"B.B.?" Mark whispered.

"Bubble Butt." I nodded toward a wavy-haired blond guy wearing a tight, black *Sticky Fingers* T-shirt rolled up at the sleeves. His Levi's clung to his plump, firm ass, and he had one hand covering his crotch. Maybe, like me, he'd gotten hard just looking at the bearded muscleman in the front row.

"Holy shit, Terry. He's got a boner!" Mark said. We both grinned like crazy but didn't dare laugh out loud.

Okay, now, talk about hot: our instructor, Ted, was Gay Stud Supreme. He reigned over his trucking court like a king over his subjects. My eyes were glued to his six-two frame, his burly chest and mammoth biceps, his well-worn Wranglers that clung to his every curve and movement. Black stubble peppered his strong jaw, and his long dark hair cascaded like an onyx river to his broad, powerful shoulders. He was one hot fucker!

I don't know how Mark and I managed to get through the three-hour class without staining our jeans over and over with hot sticky cum, but we did. Right before Ted dismissed the class, he made an announcement: "Terry, Mark, Len, and Steve…could you four stay after class a moment?"

Mark and I exchanged "What the fuck?" glances. Maybe we hadn't filled out our paperwork right or something. Yeah, or something.

The rest of the class got up and left, and the four of us—me, Mark, Mr. Meaty Meat, and Bubble Butt—made our way toward the front of the class.

"Great. Thanks for staying after," Ted said. "And welcome to G.T.C."

"G.T.C.?" I asked.

"Gay Truckers Club."

Mark and I looked at each other with big grins on our faces. The bearded guy cracked up, but the blond bubble-butted guy looked perplexed. "What the hell?" he said, in the absolute queeniest voice I'd ever heard. "What are you talking about?"

"Honey, if you're that deep in denial, go on, get out," Ted said, and the twink grabbed his purple backpack and scampered out of the room like a wounded deer.

"Okay, now that Steve's been eliminated from the equation," Ted said, rubbing his bulging crotch through his Wranglers, "that leaves just the four of us. Anyone else wanna run?"

Damn, this is crazy, I thought. *This guy cuts right to the chase.* But I went with it. I knew I'd be a fool not to.

"Hell, no," Len, the bearded stud, said, then clamped his hairy paw on his own tight package.

Mark and I stood there in awed silence.

"Good. What say we take a little field trip?" Ted headed for the door, and the three of us followed him with a skip in our step.

He led us outside to a parking lot filled with eighteen-wheelers. "All right," he told us. "In G.T.C. the primary goal is hands-on experience." He grabbed that rocket of a cock through his jeans again. "So I'm going to give you all a personal tour of a rig. Any questions?"

None of us said a word. I watched Ted's tight ass clench in his jeans as he opened the back of a big semi and hoisted himself inside. He motioned for us to follow.

Ted flicked on a light and closed the back of the truck. It was roomy inside, with a threadbare king-size mattress pushed up against the wall.

"Now for the 'hands-on' part of G.T.C.," Ted said, then

rammed his wet, fat tongue in my mouth. He turned to Mark and Len. "What are you studs waiting for? I said, 'Hands on!' "

In a second Len's beefy hands had peeled off Mark's blue T-shirt and tossed it to the floor. He pressed Mark against the metal wall of the truck and thrust his hips into my friend's crotch. Even though Mark and I had been friends for years, I'd never seen him without a shirt on. His chest was hard and defined, like a sculpture. A line of fuzzy dark hair trailed down his abdomen to his navel. I got incredibly turned on just looking at him.

"A-plus work, Len," Ted said, then mashed his stubbly face into mine.

My mind whirled and my cock grew hard as a board as Ted's powerful hands gripped my ass and he pushed his slobbery tongue deeper in my mouth. I heard groans of appreciation escape Mark's lips as Len stripped him naked and stroked my buddy's amazing nine-inch dick. I thought I'd lose it right then and there when I saw Len descend to his knees and take Mark's prick in his thick, macho lips. As Ted unbuttoned my jeans and shoved his hand down my briefs, I watched Mark and Len's nasty action over his shoulder. Len was sliding his saliva-dripping mouth up and down Mark's turgid cock, and my pal's head fell back in ecstasy.

I felt a little jealous. Mark and I had danced around each other for years, but neither of us had had the balls to initiate anything. He was straight-up hot, with a thin but muscular body and dark curly hair. Right then I swore, come hell or high water, I'd get my swollen cock in his sexy, wisecracking mouth before we left the rig.

Ted helped me pull off my jeans, then tugged gently at the patch of dark pubes that sat above the waist of my boxers. My hard cock tented my shorts, and Ted stroked it through the material. He opened the pee flap and pulled out my dick, then knelt and engulfed it in his hot, wet mouth. His stubble scratched my cock as he bobbed his sexy head back and forth, sliding up and down me with precision and ease. Man, I was going to *love* being a trucker—even if I never even got behind the steering wheel.

I had a clear view of Mark and Len as Ted expertly sucked and licked my swollen prick. Len's mouth had engulfed Mark's cock, and Mark's hands were on either side of the guy's chiseled face, guiding the hot bear back and forth. "Aww, fuck!" Mark cried out. "Aww, fuck! Suck me hard, you fuckin' stud!"

"That's it, Len. Give it to him good! Remember, you're being graded on this," Ted laughed. "And so are you, Terry," he added with a sly grin as he looked up at me and then went back to polishing my knob with his wet mouth.

Len pulled back and zeroed in on Mark's nuts, taking the bloated things in his mouth and rolling them around. Just watching those two sent more blood rushing to my cock, further filling up Ted's hot, nasty kisser. He pulled back and flicked his tongue under the rim of my cock head, and I groaned in pleasure. I grabbed his head and pumped my cock into his mouth. His long hair was coarse and sweaty, and it brushed up against my sensitive balls as he slurped on my pecker, searching out every nuance with his tongue and lips.

Ted worked that thing like a pro while Len pulled off his sweaty T-shirt and peeled off his jeans and briefs. His prick was thick, long, and hard as hell. It pointed in the air like a predator sniffing for prey, and I knew Mark's sweaty bunghole would be its feasting grounds.

Ted pulled himself off me for a moment and inserted a cassette into a stereo in the corner. As he did, my cock ached for his mouth. In fact, it felt downright abandoned without Ted's hot, wet lips on it, dripping with his hot, wet slobber. He looked to be a good fifteen years older than me, and I longed to be taught a few new tricks by this hot, gay, trucker stud. I could tell he'd been around the block—or down the highway, as the case might be—a few times, and so could my hungry, horny cock and my quivering butthole.

As Leo Sayer's "Easy to Love" blared from a couple of dusty speakers, the hot trucker faced me and stripped down to the nude, flinging his brown suede vest, white T-shirt, and jeans into a corner. My jaw dropped and my eyes bulged as I took in his broad hairy chest and big, fat pecs, his dark-brown nipples standing at attention. Thick swirls of hair covered his tanned body from head to toe, and his huge cock was full and hard. He clamped a big hand over the massive thing and stroked it back and forth. With his other hand he tugged gently at his furry, low-hanging balls. I heard Mark howl like a hyena behind me, but I couldn't peel my eyes off Ted's hot, hairy body to see what was going on—or in.

Stroking his engorged rod, the stud came toward me. I was a little nervous. I'd messed around with plenty of guys in the Navy, but Ted was a different creature altogether. A tried-and-true top, I could tell. Would I be able to take whatever he was planning on giving me? As my cock jerked, my aching butthole cried, *Yes!*

This whole scene was absolutely mind-blowing. When I woke up that morning, no way could I have predicted the crazy scene that would go down later that day in the back of that big ol' rig.

"Mr. Hopkins, I hope you're ready for a long haul," Ted said, then licked his lips. "Because my cock is ready to pound your ass." My mind broke his movements down into frames, as if we were in a movie playing at the slowest speed possible.

He came toward me and yanked down my boxers, then gently pushed me toward the mattress. "How do you want it?" he said with a million-dollar smile.

"From behind," I told him. I looked over at Mark and his hot piece of trucker meat. Len was banging Mark's ass like there was no tomorrow, and Mark was crying out like a crazed gay banshee. My cock got so hard I thought it would explode right then and there.

I got down on the mattress, pulled off my T-shirt, and rolled over. I turned my head a bit to see Ted lathering up his long, fat cock with some lube from out of a grimy bottle. Well, at least that would help ease that big ol' thing up my ass.

I closed my eyes, feeling like a little kid at an amusement park, scared as hell but thrilled, too. All of a sudden I felt Ted's sweaty, hairy chest on my back. His hands were on either side of my body, pushing into the mattress. He slid his body up and down mine, and I felt his greasy cock on my buttcheeks, in my crack, and finally poking around my hole. Ted leaned down and licked my shoulders and the back of my sweaty neck. It sounds crazy, but there was something romantic and tender about the way he moved over my body, something sensual and sweet yet raw and powerful.

I reached underneath and grabbed my dick and started stroking, which was kind of difficult with the weight of Ted's body on me. He helped me up a little, and soon I was on my knees with my legs spread wide, my left arm pressing into the mattress while I pumped my cock with my right hand.

Soon I felt Ted's monster pecker poke into my hole again. He started slowly, just teasing me at the edges, then prodding inside. I felt my aching hole expand to let him inside, and then I felt his fat cock just a couple of inches in there. Oh, God, it felt good. I hadn't had a cock inside me in a while, and my quivering hole ate it up like manna from heaven.

Ted slowly slid his pole inside me, back and forth, back and forth, and suddenly I felt his furry balls slap gently against my ass. He picked up the pace, and I pumped my cock furiously.

"Oh boy, you've got a sweet ass," Ted said. "It's fucking delicious."

Just then I heard Mark cry out in ecstasy as Len yelled, "Take it! Take it like a man!" Mark growled and screamed and used all kinds of expletives—some of which even I'd never heard before. And remember, I'd been in the Navy.

Ted kept pounding my ass, his fingers digging into my shoulders, sweat dripping off his chest and tickling my ass and lower back. I felt dizzy and feverish, and my butthole clamped down on his prick even harder. I thought I could die right there and be a happy man. Wait, no, I still had to get Mark's sweet kisser on my prick.

Well, just when I was thinking about that, all of a sudden I felt a hand reach down and pull my hand off my prick. I looked down to see Mark grin up at me and then run his sweet tongue over the tip of my cock. I wasn't about to stop him. As Ted kept ramming me from behind, Mark slurped on my prick. I braced myself on the mattress with both hands. I looked over my shoulder to see Len jacking off in the corner as he greedily watched the whole scene.

Man, this was the life.

"Yeah, get that cock all the way down your throat, Mark," Ted said. "Swallow it up." Considering the position we were in, that feat seemed impossible, but Ted's commands were sexy and fun. "You eat that boy's meat and you'll pass this course with flying colors. And while you're at it, grab your cock and start pumping."

Mark milked my pecker good and hard. Damn, if I'd known

he was such an expert at giving head, I'd have skipped all the formalities and hooked up with him a long time ago.

"Aww, fuck!" I yelped. "Fuck, fuck, fuck...I'm gonna come." Actually, I was about to cover the whole interior of the rig with my hot cream.

"I'm 'bout to blow, too," Ted echoed. And then I felt his hot, heavy spunk gushing into me like water from a fire hose.

Well, that was just too much for me to take. Right then I unloaded a fucking gallon of jizz into Mark's kisser. I looked down to see cum dribbling all over his handsome face. He licked his lips, then propped himself against the rig wall and planted long sweet kisses all over my mouth. I tasted my cum on his lips, in his mouth. Ted moved in on us, and soon the three of us were making out, our tongues darting in and out of each other's hot, sweaty, spunk-dripping mouths.

I guess Len felt left out, because he came over and stood above us. He was jerking that hot cock of his over and over, a ravenous expression glazing his eyes. Suddenly a hot, white shower hit Ted, Mark, and me, bathing us in Len's creamy hot cum as he cried out, "Gay Truckers Club! Yeeee-haw!"

The three of us laughed and laughed as Len joined us on the mattress.

And then we started in on each other all over again.

Thank God this class runs six weeks, I thought as I took Mark's beautiful cock in my mouth and Len and Ted descended on my swollen balls and aching ass.

THE LOST EXIT

Adam Kozik

The summer I turned eighteen, I decided to hitchhike from Chicago to New York, where I planned to meet a buddy in Manhattan. From there we'd hitch together to Texas and then spend a few weeks roaming around Mexico. I had a hundred bucks in my pocket and didn't owe a dime to anyone. Most of the trip was easy, with a slow, panoramic view of the American landscape. I'd gotten as far as Interstate 80, between Toledo and Youngstown, where a trucker had dropped me off at a diner. I gobbled down a quick breakfast of dried-out bacon and runny eggs before I started out again.

It was just after dawn, and as I stood on the side of the highway the pink hue of the morning sky turned to clear blue. Rig after rig passed me, but no one stopped. By the time noon rolled around, the asphalt rippled with heat waves. I peeled off my shirt and stuffed it inside my knapsack. Finally, a trucker pulled his semi over to the side of the road. NIGHT RIDER was detailed in purple letters on the side of the cab. I climbed in without even asking where the guy was going. The inside of the cab was big, and it felt strange sitting up so high.

"Sorry I'm so sweaty," I said.

His rig was one of those newer, deluxe models, and I was nervous about messing up the upholstery. The guy seemed to brush it off easily.

"I've been traveling alone for a week now," he said. "Glad to have the company."

He told me he was headed to the next truck stop, a good place to take a shower, grab a bite to eat, and sleep for a few hours. He added that he had a full-size bed in back of his cab. He was older than me and slim, with long brown hair and a goatee. He was shirtless, too, and his torso was smooth, covered in the ink of colorful tattoos. He shifted the truck's gears, and we pulled out onto the interstate.

The guy didn't say much, no more than he had to. I didn't even know his name. I suppose I didn't need to know. I'll just call him "Randy." Randy smoked grass, I could tell. The smell of the stuff permeated his cab. He swore a few times at cars that passed his truck. After a while he asked me where I was headed. I told him about my plan to meet my buddy in New York then head down to Mexico.

"Tijuana girls," is all he said.

I told him it would be a long shot to find a whorehouse and a prescription for penicillin in the same place. He laughed and said he liked me. I laughed too as I looked down at his crotch. He had a huge bulge stuffed inside his faded jeans. He was a good-looking man, but it was impossible to tell if he was gay or straight.

"Do you get high?" Randy asked me after we'd been silent for a while.

I laughed. "Yeah, I get high."

He lit a joint and passed it to me. It was a fat one, and it tasted good. Randy and I passed it back and forth, taking deep tokes, saying nothing. Soon we were both comfortably stoned, and the natural landscape appeared even mightier as we drove on in the early afternoon. Warm air blew through the cab against my face and across the damp hairs under my arms.

Randy turned his head and looked at me. I blinked. Without realizing it, my eyes got lazy over his bulge. He gave a quick grunt, and I looked out my window and kept my mouth shut. Eventually I relaxed enough to enjoy the ride once more. This was the life out here, with the trees and the mountains, the blue sky, and the open road waiting to take anyone where he wanted to go.

I listened to the big engine of the truck hum underneath us, and I finally fell asleep. I dreamed I was swimming naked in the ravine back home. I was floating on my back, looking up at the clear blue dome of sky. The sun played on my face, and I let the water buoy me with every breath.

I woke to the sound of shifting gears. Beads of sweat glistened on my chest and arms, cool on my skin. I sat up and looked at Randy. "I'm a lightweight," I told him. "Good shit."

His smile grew wide, and his long brown hair blew across his face. A trickle of sweat ran from his armpit down his torso. Just looking at it turned me on. His skin was deeply tanned, but he had a line of pale skin around his waist. From there, small dark curls caught the light before disappearing under his jeans. Again I looked at the bulge in his pants, but I didn't focus there or do anything else that might let him know I was queer.

There was a look of contentment in his eyes—the look people get when life slows down and everything comes into focus, while the whole body breathes and every hue of the sky is alive and awake.

I had a feeling Randy knew a lot of things. There was something different about him. He seemed to notice things more than most people do. His backyard was everywhere while he was in his rig. The landscape was his picture window. He looked like a man who was living life on purpose. He was free. I wanted to understand him just as much as I wanted to see the big package inside his faded jeans.

We exited the interstate just after crossing the state line. I don't remember which truck stop we pulled into. The afternoon sun was at its peak, and the truckers were parked in diagonal rows, with ten or fifteen rigs side by side.

"We'll hit the showers first," Randy said as he shifted the gears and pulled into park. He picked up his CB and called out to a handle named "J.T." A man's voice crackled over in response. Randy said words like "cotton picker," "good buddy," then said something about "back quiet" before he signed off.

I didn't say anything, possibly because I felt excited, waiting and wondering if I'd get a glimpse of Randy's dick in the shower. I'd heard about truckers who came to truck stops for more than a slice of pie. I grabbed my bag and dug inside it, pulling out my crumpled T-shirt to put on. I climbed down from the rig and followed Randy to the big plaza.

"These are some of the best showers around," he said, leading me through a door.

Looking back now, I realize it was a truck-stop shower frequented by gay men. Of course, whoever built it had intended it to be used for straights as well as gays. But what made it different was how it was possible to go into the men's showers without using any other entrance. Unlike most truck stops, where you cross through a main area, this one had its own side door, way in the back of the plaza.

Since the town itself had to be small, and the times being

what they were back then, nobody seemed to question what was going on in the men's showers. Then again, maybe they did but just didn't do anything about it.

The shower area had four large stalls divided by tiled partitions, along with a small changing space. It was clean, well maintained, and smelled like disinfectant. The place was empty except for a trucker who was getting dressed. He was a big guy and looked us over casually, without saying a word, as he zipped up his pants. Randy and I set down our things in the changing area, and I pulled my only towel out of my knapsack. I noticed the smell of sweat under my arms. The trucker finished dressing and gave us both a thumbs-up before he left.

Randy stood next to me and unbuckled his leather belt. From somewhere close I heard the sound of running water. I pulled my jeans down past my knees, then noticed Randy move closer to me. He pulled off his shirt, then unbuttoned his fly. When he reached down to scratch his tight abs, I saw a trail of hair curling down from his navel. His plump cock and saggy balls flopped from the open denim.

I stuffed my sweaty clothes inside my knapsack. Randy had already pushed his faded 501s to his ankles. I tried to check him out without being obvious, but I think he noticed me looking. As he tilted his head back, I caught a full glimpse of his naked body. Slowly he reached down with one hand and scratched his thigh. Was he teasing me? I couldn't tell. My breath caught in my throat. Even though I'd fantasized about something like this for years, now that the moment had finally arrived I was nervous as hell.

I turned to go to the showers, then quickly turned back. "Hey, do you have any soap I can use?" I asked. I had purposely left my own bar in my knapsack.

"Sure. Just don't drop it in the shower." He laughed and

handed me a fresh bar still in its package. "You know what they say."

Well, here goes nothing, I thought. Randy was sitting on the bench, taking off his socks. I reached for the soap, then slid my hand toward my crotch and, moving my hand under my balls, scratched them lightly. As I tugged my ball sac up, the head of my swelling cock was close enough for Randy to touch.

This was a bold move on my part, one that could seriously blow up in my face. At first he looked away, but then he peered up at me, giving me the same look I'd given him earlier in the truck. I felt the blood rush to my face.

His huge balls hung loosely between his legs. My cock was semi-erect. He gave me a strange, intense glare, then quickly looked at my crotch. I waited for him to say something. He stepped up to me and put his hands on my waist. His prick grew big and hard, standing straight up, rigid and ready. It bounced around for a second then steadied. Randy's blue eyes burned into me. I looked back at his hard prick. It was beautiful and huge, extremely thick at the base, with bulging veins wrapping around its girth. I reach out and grabbed it.

At that moment, I heard the door open, and I quickly took a step back as a trucker walked in, giving us both the eye. Randy was cool, picking up his towel and holding it in front of him, motioning to me with his eyes to follow him. I fumbled briefly, then turned again to look at the guy who had come in as I reached for my crumpled towel on the floor. For a second I forgot I was naked, and I scratched my nuts, giving the guy a peek at my hard-on. He glared at me intensely as I walked past him to the showers.

Before I knew it, I was standing in the shower stall, warm water splashing over my body. I was euphoric, intoxicated by the steam and letting the water spill over my head. Randy was in the shower stall next to mine. I couldn't see him because of the partition, but I heard the water running and him moving around under it.

The trucker who had walked in was in clear sight. I looked at him more closely: he exuded so much raw sexuality that my dick grew rock hard. He shrugged out of his shirt, unbuckled his belt, popped the top buttons of his pants, and leaned back. The stud ran a hand down his hard belly and pushed his pants to the floor. Just imagining this guy watching me as I touched Randy's sweaty cock made me want to shoot my load right then.

After a few moments the guy, who was now completely naked, walked toward us. He stepped up to Randy's stall and made a quick grab inside. He turned away with a smirk on his face, and after a moment I heard the spray of the third showerhead.

I shut off the tap, grabbed my towel from the hook, and left my stall. Out of the corner of my eye, I saw Randy and the trucker showering as I padded over to the changing area.

"Hey, do you have that soap I gave you?" Randy called out to me.

I realized I'd left the soap in a metal dish back in the shower stall. Without wrapping the towel around my waist, I went back, got the soap, and stepped up to Randy as he showered. He reached out and drew me toward him. I didn't know what was happening until the other trucker stepped up to me from behind, close enough to touch. Randy pushed into me. Our chests rubbed against each other and our cocks collided. He took my head in his hands and ran his fingers through my wet hair. My body shook under his spell. His hard cock slipped under my hairy balls while the other trucker spread my ass wide with both his hands.

Randy looked over my shoulder. "After you suck him, J.T., you're going to suck me too, right?"

The guy's voice was low and calm. "Maybe I'll take you both at once."

J.T. was the guy Randy had talked to back in the truck on his CB. Despite my surprise, my hard-on showed no signs of abating. It flopped from side to side, hard and ready for action. Randy stared boldly into my eyes. He drew his face toward mine and covered my mouth with his, tongue-kissing me deeply. He smelled more of Randy than of soap. He spread his legs and thrust his cock between my hairy thighs. I gripped it there between my legs. Randy rocked his hips, and his cock ran the length of my hairy ass crack. J.T. moved his hand under Randy's cock and rubbed it against my puckered asshole.

Randy and I were still in a lip-lock, and he made a low, whimpering sound. J.T. moved between us and squatted down, then took my cock inside his mouth. It felt warm as he swallowed my cock down his throat, sliding it back out then down again. He then turned to Randy and sucked and slurped on his cock. Finally, after a few moments of J.T. going back and forth between us, I felt the tip of my cock head touch Randy's hard-on as J.T. sucked both our cocks at once.

I've felt fear when I've been somewhere I shouldn't be, and fear of getting caught red-handed, but this was an exhilarating combination of the two. Looking down, seeing J.T.'s thick thighs spread wide and his big uncut prick jutting out, did nothing to ease the pressure on my prick. I felt a spray of water against my face. I looked up and saw Randy shaking his head.

"I'm not ready to blow my load yet, J.T."

J.T. looked at Randy and stood up. I realized I wasn't the only guy here who wanted to keep his boner on. J.T. moved behind me and squatted again as he spread my asscheeks with his hands. From the first lash of his tongue against my asshole I was in heaven. I honestly could have died right then and been happy. But J.T. wanted some more action, and so did Randy.

My heart was thudding in my chest, and I was speechless. I wondered what would happen if someone came in right then. Randy, whose eyes were fixed on my cock, squatted in front of me. He reached out and stroked me, but it didn't stop there. He wrapped his lips around my cock and slid it down his throat. From behind, J.T.'s tongue-fuck was moving deeper up my hole. He reached between my legs and clasped Randy's big balls in his hand. I nearly unloaded right there.

Randy bolted upright and turned around so that now my front was facing his back, almost touching him. When he spread his asscheeks apart with his fingers, I got the idea. I let a large gob of spit drip from my mouth over the head of my cock and between Randy's asscheeks to lubricate us both. Randy leaned forward against the tile and started fingering his hole. I pressed my slippery cock against Randy's hairy chute. I pressed a little harder, and Randy nodded. I thrust, and my cock plunged in. Randy's body tensed, and then he relaxed with a low groan as pleasure washed through his body.

He spread his legs a little wider as I started fucking him with a series of slow, steady thrusts. His warm, lubricated flesh caressed each vein around my hard shaft. Randy pressed his arms up against the tile siding and gave me another glimpse of his armpits, the hair clinging in damp clumps. I pummeled Randy's ass harder, pumping deep inside, my engorged cock straining in pleasure.

J.T. got up and stood alongside us, playing with his big prick as he watched Randy and me fuck. Randy began moving in time with my thrusts, and I braced both my hands on his hips, tilting his hot ass farther up while pumping my cock inside. Randy groaned as the ring of his asshole tightened and contracted around my cock. Finally he dumped his load, blasting bucket after bucket of cum onto the stall floor.

I turned to J.T., and he nodded as he looked me in the eye. I slowly withdrew my cock from Randy and turned around. J.T. bent over, offering his hairy ass up for service. From my first thrust, I could tell J.T. had a beautiful ass. He was aggressive, rough, and his hole was on fire. Randy moved up behind me. He wrapped his arms around my chest and played with my hard nips. I felt his cock press against me, still hard, dripping the last of its fuck juice. The pleasure from my cock ran through my body like a bolt of electricity.

J.T.'s hot hole was open for business as I fucked him hard and steady. With one savage backward thrust, he grunted and locked my cock inside his ass. I wasn't far behind him as he squirted his cum all over the tile.

J.T. turned around, still crouching, and licked his way up my chest. He and Randy took turns lathering up my cock with their spit, sucking the shaft at the same time and chewing lightly on my balls. Within this all-out porn loop, I effortlessly exploded a stream of cum all over their faces. I must have spurted five or six times. Both men eagerly drained my pearly juices until I was happily spent and overwhelming ecstasy shot through me.

Randy looked at me and then back at J.T. "Man, that was one hell of a ride," he said.

"You bet. The first time I ever rode in the passenger seat," J.T. said slyly.

Everybody laughed, and we showered again, then got dressed. As luck would have it, we'd had the place to ourselves the whole time. Randy told me later he figured it'd be okay even if a trucker did walk in on us. Truckers came from all around, he said, just to use those showers.

I rode with Randy as far as the New Jersey Turnpike. After

hitching another ride from there, I was in Times Square early the next morning, right on schedule to meet my buddy and find out what other surprises the road had to offer.

SNOWSTORMS AND SANDWICHES

Owen Rabideau

S ix hours and I'd only gone fifty-eight miles. Not a good start to what was supposed to be a four-day run, starting in Albany, New York, and ending on the far, far side of Nova Scotia.

Should have expected the snow, I guess. There's a reason they call this the North Country. But this was worse than usual. Blinding, swirling flakes zipped by in every direction, blowing horizontally in front of me. The snow was piling up faster than my wipers could clear it away. Small drifts were forming on the cooler corners of my hood.

Visibility was for shit, thirty feet maybe. Normally that'd be enough to force me off the road, but nobody was around that day. I was alone on the Northway, with only the occasional squawk from the radio to let me know the world was still out there.

"I-87 is now closed from Exits 2 to 18," a static-choked announcer read. "A dangerous Northeaster is moving quickly toward the Canadian border. Substantial snowfall is expected, with accumulations between eighteen and thirty inches in higher elevations. State authorities are advising drivers to stay off the road."

I'd passed Exit 18 a while ago, which meant I was still on open road. But open road doesn't mean smooth sailing.

The snow started falling harder. I could see next to nothing, but I was about twelve miles from the next exit. Might as well keep going, I thought, although it was more a matter of rolling quickly than driving slowly.

Even so, it turned out I was going too fast. The red lights cutting through the curtain of snowflakes startled me, but not as much as the erratic spinning orange light on top and the angled length of blade sticking crazily up into the air. I came down on the brake hard, swerving right, narrowly missing the toppled snowplow by inches.

My tires scraped hard against the guardrail, shaving off stinking chocolate curls of rubber. Sparks flew but quickly died. My front tires caught in a pile of spilled sand, and the rig chugged to a shuddering stop.

"Son of a bitch!" I cried.

I hoped whoever had been driving the snowplow wasn't still in there. The last thing I wanted to do was go out into the storm, but my conscience got the better of me, and I decided to check for myself. The wind pushed hard against the cab door, but I managed to wrench it open.

The snow drove right into my body. It felt like a million knifepoints in my flesh and cut at my eyes. Half-blinded, I managed to make my way to the plow. The door was a good six feet overhead.

I jumped and managed barely to get my hands around the bottom of the first step drivers use to climb up into these big boys. With one boot braced tentatively against the knobby tire spinning in the air I got enough balance to haul myself up and grab at the door handle.

"Where'd you come from?" the driver exclaimed. He couldn't have been more than twenty-five, curly headed, blond, and pale. "Dispatch said they couldn't get nobody here till morning."

I jerked my head over my left shoulder. "Just missed running into your ass end on my way through. You'd best come with me."

"Shit." The kid laughed. "Someone runs into me, I'm not gonna feel it."

"That may be true," I admitted. "But you're gonna be a good sight more comfortable in my rig." He was surrounded by handles, levers, and two long-handled shovels. "I don't drive with so much shit in my cab."

He laughed again. The sound sent a jolt directly to my cock, but I tried to ignore it.

"All right. Let me grab my stuff." He thrust a large Thermos in my hands. "I make rotten coffee, but it's hot."

The wind damn near blew us off our feet on the way back to my truck. We wound up clinging to each other, struggling to cover the twenty feet between the two vehicles. My arms were half-frozen by the time I yanked my door open.

"Goddamn, it's cold out there," the kid said. "I should have stayed where I was."

"So why didn't you?" Knocking ice out of my mustache has never been my favorite activity. I hate the feeling of short, curly hairs snapping off at the base.

"You were too cute to ignore." The kid looked around the cab, eyes lighting up at the curtain in front of the sleeper. "And it's gonna be a long-ass night."

I shook my head, not sure what I'd just heard.

He continued, unfazed. "I'm Mike. Mike Berrell. Want some coffee?"

"Sure, I guess." Maybe the ice had worked its way into my ears, screwed up my hearing.

But his hand brushed mine when he handed me the Thermos top, brimming with steaming coffee—quick enough that it could have been accidental.

You're imagining things, I told my raging libido. Too many hours of staring into a snowstorm could make a man crazy. I gulped at the hot coffee, hoping to clear my head.

Apparently my mind wasn't as cloudy as I thought. I'd no sooner set down the cup than Mike leaned toward me. "Nothing worse than kissing frozen lips," he said, just before claiming mine.

His kiss was warm, wet, and confident. I couldn't help responding, especially with the way his tongue slid strong and heavy toward my tonsils. He tasted of coffee—strong coffee, demanding coffee that wakes you up and shakes every nerve ending into total awareness.

We broke long enough to breathe. "What the fuck?" I panted, reaching for him even as I protested.

"Don't be stupid," he said. "You know you want it. Besides, what else is there to do?"

Not much, I figured. His hands were already at the buttons of my shirt, and I was tugging at his T-shirt.

"Let's get in the back," he suggested, "where there's room to stretch out."

I shoved the curtains aside and climbed in back. He followed, positioning himself half-astride me, half-next to me. "Well, there's not tons of room," he said. "But there's plenty for what I've got in mind."

The radio squawked again. "Exits 19 through 35 are now

closed," the announcer said. "Clinton, Essex, and Warren Counties are under a state of emergency. Stay off all highways and roads." Static obscured his words, but I wasn't too interested in what he had to say anyway.

Mike opened my fly and peeled off my boxers. I was already hard, my cock arching toward the cab ceiling for half a second before it disappeared into the guy's mouth.

When I say "disappeared," I mean it. That boy gobbled down my prick like he was starving and I was the last truck-stop diner for miles. His lips had barely closed around me before they slid into my pubic hair. He did this suction twisting thing— turning his head as he pulled himself off me—that had me gasping for air.

"You'd better stop, boy, 'cuz I'm gonna lose it," I warned him. He looked at me, blue eyes bright in the gray light.

"You're gonna lose it more than once, unless I've lost my touch," he said, before returning to his work. One hand cupped my balls while the other fell heavily on my stomach.

He slurped his way back down to my balls, hitting every supersensitive spot along the way.

I put my hands over my face, unable to believe what was happening. Half an hour ago I'd almost wrecked my rig—and now I was halfway to heaven.

My orgasm took me by surprise, shooting out suddenly. Mike's mouth suddenly got very wet and very warm, but he took it all like a trouper. I don't think a single drop hit my sheets.

"Wow," he smiled, wiping his lips on the back of his forearm. "I needed that almost as much as you did." He bullied me up against the back of the cab and lay down in front of me, shedding his pants in the process.

"Now you can fuck me."

"Wait a minute," I said, half laughing. His golden-haired ass was fuzzy against my sticky cock. "I'm not as young as I used to be."

"That's okay." He snuggled against me, trapping my shaft between his cheeks. "I'm not going anywhere."

I slipped one arm over his waist and propped myself up with the other. He took my hand and repositioned it over his nipple.

Mike and I lay like that for a while, staring ahead at the falling snow, as I felt his little nub grow rock hard against my palm. I traced circles with my hand, stopping every now and again to tweak the tender flesh.

The cab was silent except for the sounds of our breathing— mine quiet, his louder, punctuated by his occasional gasps.

"How'd you come to flip your plow anyways?"

A good three inches of snow had built up against my windshield. He let another quarter-inch fall before he answered, grinding his hips against me as he spoke.

"Didn't have my mind on my work. I was daydreaming."

"About what?" I rolled that nipple, plucking it half an inch from his torso.

"About doing this. About finding some big, strong top to use me. Someone who'd put me down on my knees and work me over."

I let my hand drop to his crotch. He was hard, near to trembling with excitement.

"You don't strike me as the type to get worked over." I gave him a few gentle tugs, pulling at him the way I like to be pulled. "You seem a little too aggressive for that."

"But that's what I want..." he protested. "No one ever just takes me. They're scared they're gonna break me. I always have to go looking for it."

I abandoned his meat and spit on my palm. "Well, you found it now."

He was real tight, but he sure was eager. Slipping my head in was the worst of it, nosing past the puckered ring of his sphincter.

"God," he groaned. "Give me more."

Instinct told me to buck my hips forward, to slide all the way home, but I didn't want to do that. Instead I fed it to him inch by inch, feeling myself slip slowly into that incredible tightness. His ass was convulsed around me, squeezing and releasing.

"More," he moaned.

Still I went slowly, teasing him, widening his bowels inch by excruciating inch. He tried to fling himself back on me, but I had one hand locked on his hip. It was enough to keep him still. When he finally stopped pushing back at me and relaxed a little, I let him have the rest of it in one stroke. My balls smashed against his ass. I had to bite his shoulder to keep from screaming.

He had no such compunctions.

"Fuck, yeah! Do it now!" Somehow he twisted so I was lying on top of him, plunging my shaft into him faster and faster.

I had both feet braced against the far wall. He slid forward a bit and had to brace his hands against the side to keep from smashing his face into the cold metal. In response, his hips pivoted higher, rising to meet every stroke.

We bucked wildly, each of my plunges met by his thrusts. He was strong, and I had to hold on to keep my grip. My shoulders smashed against the ceiling more than a few times, and once I hit my head hard enough to see stars.

But still we kept at it, wrestling and fucking, sawing back and forth until it was too much friction, too much sensation, too much sex.

"Here it comes, Mike," I panted.

"Me too."

I craned my neck to see, gratified by the long, stringy ropes of passion shooting from his prick. Then I went, losing my load deep inside him.

Peeling apart was difficult. Sometimes you get so far into someone else you get scared that a good chunk of you wants to remain. But we separated, zipping ourselves back into our jeans.

We were quiet for a long time. Half the windshield was obscured by snow. The part that wasn't had gone black.

"I'd better get back over to my plow," Mike said after a while. "They're gonna come looking."

"They'll find you here," I said. "Besides, two will keep warmer than one." I couldn't help smiling. "Don't be stupid. You know you want to. What else is there to do?"

"I can think of lots," he replied. "But nothing that I can let my boss catch me doing!"

It was late next morning by the time the plow trucks came through. One driver pulled up alongside my rig, bringing his bright orange truck to a dead stop. I watched him jump down and ease his way over to my door.

"Hey," he called, "we're looking for..."

"Hey, Tom! I'm up here!" Mike yelled from behind me.

Tom's face darkened, and before I knew what happened, I was lying on my face in the snow.

I sputtered up, brushing the cold snow out of my eyes. "What's your problem?"

Tom rushed me, pinning me against the side of the rig with one thick arm. "What the hell is Mike doing with you? You'd better not have hurt him none."

"Tom!" Mike appeared behind the angry driver. "Leave him alone. He had sandwiches and offered me some. It was warmer in his cab, so I stayed there." He dropped a gloved hand on

Tom's shoulder. "Sandwiches, Tom. I couldn't come home for dinner, remember? The snowstorm and all."

"Sandwiches." Tom's eyes cooled, and he let me go. "That was right nice of you." He jerked his head toward Mike's truck. "Go get ready for me to pull you out."

Mike flashed me a smile and trudged away. "Thanks for the sandwiches."

Tom waited till Mike was out of earshot then turned back toward me. "Sorry 'bout that. He's just a kid, ya know?" He eyed me carefully and sniffed the air. "Sometimes he don't think with his right mind. Makes us all worry. Especially the boss."

Another plow truck rumbled up beside his rig.

"When the boss gets over here, you best remember it's ham sandwiches Mikey likes. Mike and me live with the boss man, capeesh? Ham sandwiches."

I remembered, especially while I was looking way up into the boss's eyes. He was a big, burly, angry man. It made it hard to believe Mike couldn't get manhandled when he wanted to—but I wasn't about to start that conversation!

From then on, though, you'd better believe that whenever I pulled my rig through the Adirondacks, I had two or three ham sandwiches in my cooler. Rain or shine, summer sun or winter snow. Hey, you never know.

GUTPUNCH

Simon Sheppard

could fucking kill you right now," I say, my hands around his throat, and the guy's dick stands straight up.

That's how it goes, usually, what I do for a living. *Tough, experienced dominant for hire,* the ad says, and I try to give 'em their money's worth. Most of my steady clientele is pretty much what you'd expect: masochists unsure of how else to get just what they want. What they need. Many of them are dweeby, or shy, or just plain unattractive. A couple of them are stressed-out executives too busy to bother cruising the leather bars. And more than a couple are married men.

All of them like to be worked over.

This particular client, who I'll call Larry, is a cute little guy who loves to be tied down spread-eagle to the bed. I kneel over him, straddling his chest, my big cock and hairy crotch so close to his face he can smell it. And I put my hands around his throat and squeeze. Works every time.

In the beginning, just feeling my big strong hands around his throat would make him shoot his load. These days, I usually have to knee his crotch as well. I'd never tell Larry, but I get off on it too, on him in particular. His vulnerability, how twisted he is, the feel of his skinny cock pulsing away against my knee.

Larry's my last client of the day, of the week in fact. He pays me well, in cash, makes a neat note of our next appointment in his pocket organizer, and sees me to the door. My Jeep is waiting in his suburban driveway. I climb in and head for home.

Back in the city, I strip off my leathers and my stained jockstrap, take a shower, and change into chinos and a nicely pressed plaid shirt. The man in the mirror still looks good—nearly forty, handsome, neatly trimmed beard, piercing eyes. I slip the silver hoops from my earlobes; Dad never did like my earrings. Little does he suspect what I do for a living.

Four-thirty. If I drive straight through, I should be at my father's house in time for night-before-Easter dinner. Not that I believe in that religious stuff, but he does, and since Mom passed on he's been pretty much all alone. So for the last few years I've thrown a good canned ham in the back of the Jeep and headed for the house I grew up in.

It's interstate most of the way, easy to make good time. As I leave the edges of the city, the sun's last traces vanish from view. It's been a colder-than-normal spring and there's still plenty of snow. The full moon makes the open fields gleam bright white.

I'm still a good sixty miles from my hometown, out in the middle of nowhere, farmland all around, when my eyes start to close. A rough, mostly sleepless Friday night is beginning to catch up with me, and the endless miles of white nothingness aren't helping matters. I manage to keep my eyes propped open for fifteen minutes or so, praying for a cup of coffee, till the next exit comes into view. To my relief, a big, bright neon sign announces the Palm Tree Diner. Palm Tree? Somebody sure as hell had a Midwestern sense of humor.

I pull into the parking lot. A few cars, a couple of RVs, a semi. The diner's one of those old-style streamline jobbies that seem to have vanished everywhere, only to reappear as trendy theme restaurants in hip city neighborhoods. This one's the genuine article, though, and someone's actually carried through the palm tree theme. A neon pink flamingo over the door, a mural of a Hawaiian beach scene, and damned if the waitress isn't wearing a lei over her starched green uniform. This would be surreal even if I weren't so woozy. I slouch down into a booth somewhere in the general vicinity of Diamond Head.

"Coffee, hon?" asks Erma the tropical waitress.

"Black."

"Getcha anything else?" She has a little Easter bunny pinned to her lapel, next to her name tag.

"Let me see a menu, please." I feel like adding "Mom."

She's back in a shot with the menu and a cup of not-bad coffee. I peruse the specials—the Waikiki Burger, the Eggs Aloha —and settle for a slice of lemon meringue pie. It's not till I'm biting into the pie's tart sweetness that I notice the guy facing me from two booths down. Latino, Mexican, whatever. Dark brown skin, glossy black hair, mustache. Not particularly good-looking, a little tough maybe. And he's staring straight at me. I can't read his look, but at first I figure it's hostility; I don't think I look particularly gay when I'm walking down a city street, but out here who knows? If I stare back, he'll take it as *my* hostility. But if I avoid his eyes, he'll think it's a sign of weakness. Either way, I lose.

He takes a bite of his club sandwich, never taking his eyes off me. Mayonnaise squishes out onto his mustache. He puts the sandwich down, sticks his tongue way out, and slowly, deliberately licks his mouth clean. The effect is unexpectedly lewd. I look around to see if anyone else has noticed. Senior citizens, families with kids, Erma, they all seem totally oblivious. I look back, part my lips slightly, and stick out just the tip of my tongue. The ghost of a smile crosses my new friend's dark face. And then he winks. Boy, did I read him wrong.

Eyes still locked on mine, he picks up his napkin, wipes his mouth, and rises from the booth's Naugahyde seat. He's short, kind of squat, maybe powerfully built. And there's a bulge at the crotch of his jeans.

He walks over my way, squeezes his dick for just a fraction of a second, and then strolls right by. I don't care if I'm being obvious, I turn my head to see where he's gone.

The men's room.

I wait just long enough to make it seem like it could be a coincidence, and then I get up and follow him to the can. It's not till I'm standing that I register that I've popped a hard-on, too, so I hurriedly pull out the tails of my plaid shirt and hope nobody's watching too closely. The women's room sign reads WAHINES. The men's is just plain GENTS. Gents it is.

He's standing there at a urinal, of course, and he turns his head when he hears the door swing open. One of those trucker's wallets, the kind with the chain, is in his back left pocket. Must be his semi in the lot outside. There're just two urinals; he watches me wordlessly as I walk over beside him and pull down my fly. I watch him stroking his hard, brown, uncut dick as I try to maneuver my own stiff meat out of my pants. At last, hard-on in hand, I look up, at his face. The flirtatious look is gone. "You want to suck my dick, fag," he says. It's not a question, it's a statement. And he's right. I nod. "Say it," he snarls. "Say 'I want to suck your dick.' "

"I want to suck your dick." My mouth is dry. "Please."

He walks into the bathroom's one stall, turns, and leans up against the stained metal wall, eyes half-closed, playing with his long, dark foreskin. I follow him in and shut and lock the door. I look into his cold, brown eyes and reach for his Latino cock. He knees me in the groin. I gasp. I want to hit back. I don't.

"On your fucking knees," he snaps. "Your mouth is all I'm interested in."

One hand on the filthy toilet bowl, I lower myself to the tiled floor and wrap my lips around his short, fat prick. I can smell his crotch, taste his cheese. He grabs the back of my head and slams himself all the way into my throat. "You faggot," he whispers. "You *like* this, don't you?" He shoves me around till I'm backed up against the door and thrusts hard, slamming my head into the metal door again and again. His dick may not be very long, but it's thick enough to make me gag. I try to back off of it. He slaps my face. "You eat that fucking dick, faggot," he says, cruelly, urgently. And he brings his hand down again, harder, hard enough to make me wince.

What have I got myself into? I'm thinking, when the restroom door opens. The two of us freeze. Whoever it is tries the locked door, then walks over to a urinal and pisses. I can hear his hot pee splash against the stained white porcelain. He leaves, without flushing or washing up. *People sure are slobs,* I think, somewhat inappropriately.

The beefy trucker is stuffing his dick back in his jeans. "I can think of a better place to do this." He's already pushing me aside and walking out of the toilet stall. "You coming with me, fag?"

On his way out of the diner, he drops some money on his table. I leave a ten-dollar bill on mine. I guess I wouldn't mind Erma the tropical waitress thinking of me as a big tipper, but mostly I just don't want trouble. I follow him through the icy parking lot, toward his big truck. I've never had sex in a semi before, and I'm having fantasies of eating his cum in the cab of the truck, but the Latino guy keeps on going, past his truck, out of the lot, into the moonlit, snowy field behind the diner. I'm starting to get a little scared, but my dick's still hard, so I follow. We reach a little bunch of trees. He stops, turns, and smiles. It's not a friendly smile.

"You *are* a faggot, a hungry cocksucker, following me out here like this."

He's right, but he's also wrong. I may be a hungry cocksucker, but I'm not his faggot. I'm nobody's faggot. "Fuck you," I spit back.

He hits me. He hits me in the head. I see stars, literally see stars. I've never seen stars before, not like this. I'm thinking, *Now I know where they got that figure of speech, "seeing stars,"* when he hits me again. I hit back. Punch him in the gut. He punches back, not hard enough to do real damage but hard enough to hurt.

And hard enough, it turns out, to make my still-hard cock throb with desire. I do what I know will piss him off the most: I grab hold of his jacket, pull him toward me, and kiss him hard on the lips. I can feel his glossy black mustache against my upper lip; taste the bacon, lettuce, and tomato on his breath; feel his hard basket rubbing against my thigh like a horny dog humping a bitch in heat. His fist thumps into my belly again. I shove my tongue into his mouth. He resists, opens his lips for a second, then pulls his face away.

"You fag," he says, but some of the anger is gone from his voice, replaced by I-don't-know-what. For one long moment we stand there face-to-face in the cold, crisp night, the headlights of distant passing cars casting sweeping beams through the trees.

Two hard, horny men in the middle of nowhere.

Then he shoves me. I slip on the snowy ground, fall down. But I'm still grabbing his jacket and he comes down with me. We roll on the snow, half dry-humping, half wrestling for supremacy. I grab at his shirt and it rips open, revealing a gold crucifix nestled in the thick black hair of his chest. Improbably, the full moon's light catches the cross, a golden glint in the icy night. Then he forces me over onto my back and pins my wrists above my head. He's a lot smaller than I am, but the motherfucker is strong. One knee pries apart my thighs and he gets his legs between mine. I strain upward, my crotch jamming into his. The snow is fucking cold.

"The only question tonight," I say, "is who screws who."

"No question about that," he says calmly, and spits in my face. He's right. "You ready?"

I nod. He lets go of my wrists, gets onto his feet. I struggle up, walk over to a tree, face the trunk, and unbuckle my pants. "Just one request," I say, holding up the condom I always carry in my jacket pocket.

"Don't worry," he says, grabbing it. "I ain't gonna let no faggot give me nothing."

I feel a hand on my waistband. He pulls down my chinos, which fall to my ankles. He grabs my briefs and tears at them till they give way with a ripping sound. The night wind, which has been cold against my flesh, feels astonishing against my hot, hard cock. I lean into the tree and spread my legs as far as my pants will let me. I hear him spit, feel his fingers working his saliva into my hole. The head of his thick cock presses into me. I don't know if I'm relaxed enough to let him in. Doesn't matter; he gets in anyway. It hurts, but not that much. *He's a man. He's entitled to this.* The bark is rough against my arms, the wind is cold against my thighs, his dick is hot inside me. He slaps my butt a couple of times and I push my ass out for more.

"Nice cunt," he says. I take it as a compliment. And then he starts screwing me for real. My guts open up for him and he pumps into me like it's the last fuck of his life and he's gonna make the most of it. I don't know how much longer I can take it, being abused by this powerful little fuck-machine. He throws his left arm around my throat and arches me backward. "I'm coming, faggot," he says urgently. "I'm coming, buddy." His arm presses into my windpipe and I feel blood pounding in my head. He pumps harder, grunts, and punches my gut. He yells in some unknown language, and rams into me again and again, slamming his right fist into me with every thrust.

He takes his arm away, stands there for a minute, then pulls his dick out of me. My ass is still pulsating. "Mind if I come?" I gasp.

"Suit yourself," he says, and within seconds I jack myself to climax, shooting big wads of spunk onto the even-whiter snow. I wipe the last bits of cum onto my hand and lick it clean. When I bend over to pull up my pants, I can barely keep my balance.

I turn around to look at him. He's using the rag that was my briefs to wipe himself off. Then he pulls his jeans back up over his hairy, muscled thighs.

"C'mon," he says, and we walk off side by side, leaving a used condom lying amidst a welter of snowy footprints.

He leads me to his waiting truck. He gets into the cab, unlocks the passenger-side door and says, "Hop in." He reaches into the glove compartment and pulls out a bottle. Jim Beam. "Have some." I take a swig and offer it to him. "Nah. I got an all-night run. And I was thinking about going to midnight mass. If I take anything, it'll be something to help me keep awake."

I'm sitting there, drinking bourbon, looking out at the snowy night, when I notice a photo taped to his dashboard. A woman and two young girls. He doesn't have to tell me. His wife and daughters.

There's nothing more to say. I put the bottle back and open the truck door. "Happy Easter, buddy," he says. I reach over and squeeze his thigh, then jump down out of the cab. I walk over to my Jeep and don't look back.

FUCKED AT THE TRUCK STOP

Christopher Pierce

I had lots of adventures on my cross-country move from Los Angeles to Sparkling Springs, Florida. This is one of them.

With one hand on my crotch and the other on the steering wheel, I drove through the night. A breeze blew in through my car's open windows, whispering through my hair and soothing my skin, which was hot from a long, sweaty day on the road.

But no breeze could cool the heat between my legs, a heat that grew stronger with every passing moment. I felt myself through the thin fabric of my shorts, loving the sensation of my cock hardening beneath my fingers. It stretched to its full length until it strained against my shorts.

I glanced down and saw a small wet spot where a drop of precum had oozed out through the fabric. I rubbed my erect penis from its base to its bulbous head, savoring the extra friction achieved by the layer of cloth between it and my hand. It felt great, but fondling myself while I drove wouldn't tame the fire in my crotch.

The road stretched out ahead of me, the broken lines that cut it in half down the middle streaking together into a glowing smear of yellow. My headlights illuminated the terrain ahead, even though there was nothing to see.

Barren, featureless land surrounded me. Every fifty miles or so there might be a town, so small I was through it and out the other side in five minutes.

I needed to rest.

And get my rocks off.

A sign appeared on the horizon: TRUCK STOP—NEXT EXIT. That sounded good. I could park in a dark corner, jerk myself off, then sleep for a few hours.

I pulled off at the next off-ramp and followed the signs to the truck stop. It was in a wooded area, a large flat parking lot with a big restroom building and a small twenty-four-hour convenience store at one end. In front of the store there were a few semis but no cars.

I parked my car up front of the restroom, realizing it had been several hours since I'd pissed. But how was I going to piss with this massive hard-on?

I got out of the car and walked awkwardly inside the building. The restroom was big, with lots of stalls. I headed for the long piss trough against the wall. I pulled my shorts down, and my cock popped out, hard as a board.

I closed my eyes and willed it to go down.

Relax, I told myself. After a few minutes my dick was soft enough for me to pee, and with a happy sigh I released my bladder and let my urine flow freely. When I was done, I stuffed my cock back in my shorts and turned around.

I wasn't alone.

Against the back wall, leaning casually with his arms folded, stood a man. He was older than me, probably in his mid thirties, and was dressed like a working man, with a flannel shirt, dirty jeans, and hiking boots. His jaw was darkened with several days' growth of beard. An old baseball cap was perched on his head.

He stood there grinning at me.

"Hey," I said, trying to cover my surprise.

"Hey, yourself," he said.

"I didn't know anyone was watching."

"Yeah." The man nodded. "I didn't expect to find anyone in here this late either. I just came in to piss."

I couldn't stop my eyes from dropping from his face to his crotch. The denim there was well worn—rubbed white and nearly threadbare. The outline of his cock was clearly visible. My tongue slipped out of my mouth and wet my lip.

"Can I...watch?" I asked suddenly.

"Watch me piss?" he said. "Sure, I guess so."

I stepped to the side, and the sexy man walked over to the trough. He undid his belt and pulled his meat out of his pants. It was hot—big and full even though it was soft, with a big dark head and veiny shaft. He took his dick in one hand and aimed it into the trough. A stream of piss shot out, and the sound of it hitting the porcelain and flowing into the drain echoed in the big empty restroom.

The man closed his eyes and tilted his head back a little as he pissed. "Aaahhh..." he murmured in relief and pleasure. "Want to touch it?" he asked.

"Yes," I said simply.

"Then go ahead."

Before he'd even finished the sentence I'd reached out and grasped that succulent piece of meat in my hand.

"You like that?" the trucker asked.

"Yeah..." I whispered.

"You like holding my big fat cock?"

"Yeah..."

He turned to face me, letting me continue to hold his dick in my hand. I felt it start to get hard. It was such a great feeling, so hot.

"You wanna do more than hold it, don't you?" the man asked.

"Yes," I told him.

"Then do it. Get down on your knees and suck it like you want to."

I obeyed and dropped down to my knees in front of him. As I opened my mouth and closed my eyes, the guy shoved his cock between my lips. I clamped my mouth around it, thrilling to the feeling of it growing inside me, filling me with its strength and power.

He started to face-fuck me, pushing his dick deep into my mouth, pulling it back until it was almost all the way out, then shoving it back in again. I didn't care if someone might walk in. I didn't care about the hard floor digging into my knees. I didn't even care that my own stiff cock was staining my underwear with new precum and begging to be stroked. All that mattered was sucking this man's dick and doing it as best I could.

"Mmm...that's great," he growled above me. His voice moved through me, and it was as if my blood responded to his pleasure, heating up and rushing through my veins. I wanted to push him over the edge, to make him feel better than he ever had before.

"I'm gonna come, man," he said. "Ready for me to shoot?"

I took my mouth off his cock to answer him. "Yeah! I want to see you come!"

I put my face back down between his legs and licked his balls. They smelled fantastic—sweaty and musky from their owner's long day on the road. They tasted just as good, and I massaged them with my tongue, gently taking one ball into my mouth to roll it lovingly inside. As I did, the trucker jerked himself off, pumping his cock in his fist. Suddenly he shifted a little and aimed his dick into the piss trough.

"This is it!" he said. "I'm coming, man!"

"Go for it!" I said, and as I licked his ball sac again I felt the churning liquid inside heat up and shoot down his shaft on its way out of his cock. The trucker grunted as he came, and I turned my head enough to watch his bursts of spunk jet into the trough. His body shuddered for a few seconds, and then he was done. He stuffed his cock back in his pants and zipped them up.

"That was fuckin' awesome," he said.

I stood up, rubbing my own dick through my shorts. "You're a stud," I told him. "You're fucking awesome!"

"You gettin' back on the road tonight?"

"I was going to jerk off, then catch a few hours of sleep first," I said. "Why?"

The trucker suddenly looked embarrassed, almost shy. I love it when men let themselves be vulnerable—it turns me on.

"It's okay, man," I assured him. "What is it?"

"Well," he said, "you seem like a nice guy…"

"Yeah?"

"I've been on the road almost two weeks now, and my girlfriend back home, well, she…"

"Stopped sleeping with you?" I finished. The guy looked surprised that I'd guessed right.

"Yeah," he said. "I don't know what her problem is."

"So you haven't been getting your rocks off."

"That's true," he said, "but there's more to it."

"What?"

Suddenly the trucker looked angry, and pointed at me. "If you ever tell anyone about this, I'll find you and kick your fucking ass in the dirt, understand?"

I put up my hands, laughing. "Whoa!" I said. "Take it easy! Who would I tell? This is just between us."

"Okay." He paused. "The best part of sex for me, after coming, of course, is the part after, when I get to hold her."

He paused, as if waiting for me to say something, but I just looked at him, listening.

"And tonight there's no chicks around," he went on, "and I was wondering, since you're probably a fag—"

"Gay," I interrupted.

"What?"

"Not fag. Gay. Don't say 'fag.' Especially if you want me to help you out tonight."

He looked surprised but nodded and continued. "I figured since you're gay you might..." he trailed off.

"Might what?" I prompted him. "Say it. It's cool to say it."

"Let me hold you for a while," the trucker finished without meeting my eyes. "I've got a sleeping compartment in my rig."

I smiled at him. "How about you get me off," I said, "and then you can hold me all fucking night."

"Sounds good, but I've got some buddies out there. How can I get you to my truck without them knowing what we're doin'?"

"Tell you what...you take care of me, and I'll take care of that."

I told the trucker my idea, and he agreed it was a good plan. Then he took me into one of the bathroom stalls to fulfill his end of the bargain. Inside the stall with the door closed, he grabbed me and held me tightly, my back against his chest. His left arm was wrapped around my middle, pressing me against him. His right hand grabbed my crotch through my shorts, and I jerked in surprise.

"What—?" I started to say, but the trucker clamped his left hand over my mouth, and I shut up instantly.

"Sshhhh…" he said softly in my ear. "Keep quiet, little gay boy. I don't want to share you with anyone else." My cock flexed and stiffened under his hand, and the trucker rubbed it through my shorts. Despite the order to be quiet, I couldn't prevent a little moan from escaping my lips.

"This is just what you need, isn't it, gay boy?" he whispered. "You need a real man to take care of you and get your rocks off, isn't that right?" I nodded.

The trucker stuck his right hand down into my shorts and grabbed my cock and balls in his fist and squeezed them. "You need to get fucked, gay boy?" he asked as he jacked my dick. It was intense and wild, being jerked off by a total stranger in a restroom off the open highway in the middle of the night. I nodded again. "If I take my hand off your mouth you gonna be quiet?"

"Yes, sir!" I said into his hand, and he took it off my mouth, letting it drop until it found my left nipple and pinched it hard. With his right hand he continued to play with my cock, squeezing it and jerking it.

"I'm gonna take you back to my truck, gay boy," he said, "and I'm gonna fuck you long and hard."

I nodded enthusiastically, remembering again his warning for silence. It felt so fucking good to be in his power this way, to be his prisoner. The heat in my balls was burning, and soon enough I couldn't hold back anymore. I shuddered in the trucker's arms, and he aimed my dick into the toilet bowl. My climax roared through me, and squirts of cum shot out of my cock.

"Yeah," he said. "That's it, gay boy. You need a real man to take care of you, don't you?"

I nodded again, even though I was dying to cry out in pleasure. He held me until I stopped quivering then stuffed my cock and balls back into my shorts. He opened the stall door and led me out in the empty bathroom, then turned to me with a wide grin on his unshaven face.

As we had agreed, he leaned down toward me and I let myself fall forward over his shoulder. He grabbed on to my legs and lifted me up, hoisting me like a sack of potatoes until he was standing straight up and had me slung over his shoulder.

"You okay?" he asked.

"I'm good," I told him.

"Stay real limp so they believe you're unconscious."

"Yes, sir," I said, closing my eyes. The trucker carried me out of the bathroom into the cool night air. He was strong—having a hundred-and-sixty-pound man over his shoulder didn't slow him down one bit.

It felt good to be carried like that, with his arms holding my legs tight so I wouldn't fall. In a way it was intimate, I guess. Even though what we were doing was technically playacting, it was still cool to be carried by this sexy stud. With my eyes shut I couldn't see anything, of course, but I could hear the sound of the trucker's footsteps on the concrete.

"Hey, Jim!" one of the guys said, and we stopped.

"What the hell is this?" a second voice asked.

"Found him out cold in the bathroom," my trucker said, whose name I guessed was Jim.

"Got any money on him?" a third man asked.

"Fuck you," Jim said. "I'm not a thief."

"Want me to call the cops on my radio?" the first man said.

"Naw," Jim said. "I'm gonna let him sleep in my rig till he wakes up. He might be on the run or something. I want to hear his story before I call the cops."

"He got a knife or anything on him? Might be a crazy fuckin' drug addict."

"No," Jim said, adjusting me on his shoulder. "He's clean. I can handle him. Don't worry."

"Okay, man," the second guy said. "You gonna catch some z's yourself?"

"Maybe. I wanna head out early."

"Cool. Later then."

The truckers exchanged good-byes, then Jim started walking again. After a few steps he stopped, and I heard the sound of him fishing his keys out of his pocket.

He unlocked and opened a door, then lugged me up and into what I figured was his truck. It smelled like him, thick and male, with a trace of sweat and something else that was probably beer. Jim walked a few short steps, opened another door, then took me inside and set me down on a soft surface. I was a little sorry the carrying was over, but I knew what was coming would be even better.

I heard Jim walk back and close and lock all the doors. Then he came back into the compartment he'd stashed me in and snapped on a dim light.

"They bought it," he said. "It's cool. No one can see us."

I opened my eyes. The sleeping area of Jim's truck wasn't very big, and the "bed" itself seemed tight for two men, but it would be okay. There was more than enough room for what we had in mind.

"Are you going to fuck me now?" I asked, and Jim smirked.

"Well, I sure as shit didn't carry you all this way to talk about art," he said, and we both laughed. "Take your clothes off."

I obeyed and slipped out of my shorts and T-shirt, then kicked off my shoes. The trucker pulled off his flannel shirt to reveal two nice pecs clearly showing through a thin undershirt and framed by suspenders. He unlaced his boots and took them off but left his socks on. I lay naked on the bed, looking up at the rough stud who'd carried me like I weighed no more than a bag of laundry.

Everything about him excited me. The dust on his cheeks, the sweat stains on his undershirt from driving all day, the way his cock and balls hung low in his briefs when he unhooked his suspenders and let his dirty jeans fall to the floor.

My cock got hard when I looked in his eyes and saw his hunger. Jim pulled off his undershirt, and I was hit by his sexy odor. It was just like him—striking, musky, undeniably erotic. His chest was hairy, his pecs crowned with big dark nipples. His stomach was flat and hard. His entire torso was tanned golden brown. I imagined him driving long sunny days with his shirt off, or fishing shirtless on his days off. Below his tan line he was just as sexy. His penis stood out from a bush of dark pubic hair. It was long, hard, and veiny, the big foreskin pulled back from the flared red head.

I resisted leaning forward and devouring it again as I had before. I resisted because I knew getting fucked by him would be even better than giving him a blow job.

"You look good enough to eat," the trucker said. "I like the way you look up at me."

"You look fucking awesome!" I said. "I need you to fuck me."

"Yeah? You need me to pile-drive my big cock into your little gay-boy butt?"

"Yes," I said. "Please!"

"Beg me," he said with a grin.

I turned over on my back and spread my legs wide for him. "Come on, man!" I pleaded. "I *need* you inside me! I need you to ram me, stud! Come on, man! *Please* pound me, pork me, take me, *fuck me!*"

"Now, that's what I like to hear!"

My entire body tingled and vibrated with excitement as the naked trucker crawled between my legs.

I fished a condom out of the pocket of my shorts and quickly tore it open. The trucker said nothing as I unrolled the latex sheath over his formidable meat and squeezed some lube on it from a travel-size tube in my other pocket.

"You set, gay boy?" Jim asked me.

"Yes, sir!" I said, and he placed my feet on his shoulders.

I knew this man wasn't going to be big on romantic foreplay, so I prepared myself for a direct assault. The trucker took his cock in his hand and aimed it until it was pressed against my asshole. I took a deep breath and willed my whole body to relax and receive him.

It worked a little, but when he thrust himself into me it still hurt. Still, the pain was accompanied by pleasure that was sharp and bright in its intensity.

"Oh, fuck yeah..." he said, closing his eyes as my asshole gripped his dick and held it firmly. Jim fucked me hard then, shoving himself into me savagely. It was painful and wonderful at the same time. "Aw..." he growled. "Nothin' like a little gay-boy ass."

"That's right, man," I encouraged him. "Fuck me like you want to fuck your girlfriend! Long and hard and deep. Go on, I can take it!"

"Feels so fuckin' good!"

"Yeah, stud, 'cause you're so fuckin' hot!"

His thrusts got longer and faster, and I had to anchor myself against the wall behind my head with my hands or he'd have tossed me all over the bed with the passion of his fucking.

My cock was erect and dripping from the incredible ordeal my ass endured. It was amazing to feel this way, to be reamed and pummeled by a real man, a trucker stud like Jim!

"I'm gonna come, gay boy," he said breathlessly.

"Me too," I moaned.

I thought about how he'd looked earlier, leaning against the bathroom wall, his big fat cock clearly visible through his jeans. I thought about sucking that dick, feeling his manhood and power inside me. I thought about his carrying me, how he had effortlessly hoisted me over his shoulder.

But most of all I thought about that exact moment, the sensation of this man making rough love to me, screwing me, fucking me like I'd never been fucked before.

And I came.

My load of spunk shot out of my cock in milky ropes that landed on my chest and abdomen. My orgasm hit me hard, blooming inside me like an explosive flower of ecstasy. I felt my asshole contract, tightly clenching around the trucker's thrusting dick.

"Oh, fuck YEAH!" he said, and I imagined the pleasure of the contraction sending him over the edge as my butt held him in its grasp of bliss. "I'm coming, gay boy!" he groaned above me.

"Do it, man!" I urged him. "Give me everything you've got!"

The trucker's next groan was wordless, an animal cry of passion, and with his final thrust I knew he was shooting his load deep inside me. I took it all, gratefully, wanting all he had, wanting to give him as much pleasure as I could.

Jim's hands gripped my upper arms, his fingers digging in. In that moment I didn't care about pain. All I could think of was pleasing him, making him feel better than he ever had.

And I thought, just maybe, I had.

Jim collapsed on top of me, the last waves of his orgasm washing over him and through him.

We lay there for a while, so long I thought he might have fallen asleep. But then he grunted and raised himself up, pulling his cock out of my butt, which felt suddenly empty without it. With my eyes closed I heard him snap off the condom. Then I felt something rough and dry on my chest, and I realized he was wiping my spunk off of me.

When he was done he turned off the light in the sleeping compartment and got back in bed with me. With his strong arms the trucker pulled me close, my back to his chest. He wrapped those arms around me and held me tightly. There was no need for words.

I snuggled against him and rested my head on the pillow. Only then did I suddenly remember how tired I was, and I fell asleep almost immediately, the reassuring feeling of Jim's big soft cock against my buttcheeks.

The next morning I woke up early.

The trucker was still asleep, snoring quietly with a smile of contentment on his face. I got up slowly and carefully so as not to wake him. I moved my pillow into the space I had occupied, and in a moment he was holding it tightly as if it were me.

I quietly made my way back to the truck's cab and let myself out of the passenger door, locking it behind me.

Walking back to my car, I took a deep breath of fresh morning air and was ready for the new day. A few moments later I drove out of the truck stop and headed back toward the freeway entrance, where the open highway waited for me.

TRUCKER'S LAST RIDE

Max Roper

I was tired, bone tired. I'd been driving rigs for nearly two decades, and my fiftieth birthday was just around the bend. Even though I loved life on the open road, it was getting to my body, making me stiff and sore in places I never knew I had. I've been an out, proud, gay man since I was eighteen, and even though other truckers sometimes gave me shit about it, I'd stood up for myself so many times most of them learned to respect me. My Joe Frazier right hook didn't hurt matters either.

When I told my longtime, live-in lover, Jay, that I planned on retiring, maybe opening up a stereo store in town, I'd expected him to hoot and holler in joy and celebration. After all, for the past eight years he'd been complaining about my being away from home so much. Instead he said, "Aren't you going to miss all the quick 'n' dirty fucks?"

Jay and I had fallen into a comfortable—but very hot—pattern. After a long haul, I'd come home and tell him about all

the nasty action I'd gotten at truck stops, rest stops, and sometimes on the side of the road. Often, he and I would role-play,
me being the horny trucker top pounding my cock into him, the
young hitchhiking bottom. I have a good ten years on Jay, so
our reality meshed quite well with our fantasies.

I had a feeling Jay was gonna miss my quick 'n' dirty fucks
way more than I was. Whenever I came home with a good, filthy
story, he'd peel off his clothes in no time flat, curl up in bed, and
stroke that giant cock of his while I described every last detail
of my raunchy on-the-road encounters. Don't get me wrong—I
loved hot, nasty, one-time sex, but Jay gobbled up my stories
almost as if he starred in every one of them.

"Tell you what," I said, "since next Wednesday is my last
haul, I'll make sure it's my hottest, wildest ride ever. I'm gonna
fuck some hot piece of ass so good and hard that when I come
back you'll be shooting your nasty load all the way to the Pacific
Ocean."

Jay's lips curled up in a crooked smile as he ran a hand
through his wavy blond hair. "What's your route this time?"

"Just a short run to Chicago and back. Down the I-90," I
told him.

"Make sure you pull off at that rest stop near Janesville,"
he said. "Remember that married guy from Canada who came
about a dozen times?"

"Whew, boy, do I. I'm sure the janitors had a good time
moppin' up all that spooge. Probably used a sponge the size of
a sofa."

That got a laugh out of Jay. Then all of a sudden I felt his
warm hand go down my boxers and grab my throbbing prick.

Five days later I was hauling a load of washers and dryers down
to Chicago. The July sun was raging hot, and sweat poured down

my brow. The A/C in my rig had blown out about an hour before, and by the time I pulled off at the rest stop outside of Janesville, I couldn't wait to get my mouth on something cold—well, and something hot, too. I vowed I'd make good on my promise to Jay.

As I pulled into the lot, I spotted just a few sedans and two rigs. I got out and put some change in the soda machine. When the Coke can came out, I drank the whole thing down in just a few swigs. My tight white T-shirt was drenched in sweat. I took a quick sniff of my pits—I stank to high heaven.

Twenty-five yards or so away, I saw two hot young guys—one blond and one brunet—stroll into the men's restroom. One of them squeezed the other's ass hard. Damn, they looked good. Their butts were tight in their shorts, their asscheeks clenching as they went in. I knew I was gonna have some fun with these hot guys.

I let a few minutes pass before I went into the bathroom. I stood at the sink washing up when suddenly I heard groans, then passionate words coming from the handicapped stall.

"Yeah, man, right there!" a voice cried out. "Fuckin' squeeze my nuts. Squeeze 'em good."

"Like this?" the other voice said.

"Mmm...yeah...that's it. That's it. Now suck my dick!"

I recognized that second voice right away. It was Jay! That little sneak had planned this all along. And he clearly was topping the other guy. What a change from the sexy bottom-boy I knew. What a fuckin' surprise. A fuckin' hot surprise.

Suddenly I had an idea. I pounded on the stall door, and in the deepest, gruffest voice I could muster I bellowed, "Police! This is a raid! Open up!"

The door flew open, and Jay's face took on a mock look of horror. "Oh...um...officer, hello," he said. "Umm, we were just—"

"I know what you little faggots were doing." A brunette head peeked up from the snout of Jay's rock-hard, precum-dripping rod. It was our next-door neighbor, Tony. Damn! Right then I wondered if Jay and Tony fucked each other silly whenever I was on the road. I wasn't jealous, though—I only wished I'd gotten some of Tony's sweet ass first! He was in his mid twenties and worked in construction. Hell, I didn't even know the guy was gay.

"Hello, Officer Roper," Tony said in a meek voice, though he knew right away I was his neighbor and not a cop. "I'm sure you can overlook this slight indiscretion. I mean, if we give you a little something in return." He gave me a sexy wink.

"Hell, yeah, kid," I growled. "You're gonna give me some of that tight ass while you suck my boy Jay's fat cock."

I could tell Jay just about shot his wad right there and then. A sly smile crept across his angelic face, and the thick purple head of his penis seemed to expand two inches. I reached out and caressed its veiny shaft, then gave Jay a little nibble behind the ear.

"Good goin', doll," I whispered so only he could hear. I entered the stall and locked the door behind me.

Tony peeled off his shirt, and I gave him the once-over. Fuck, he was hot. He was an Italian stallion, with dark sweat-soaked locks that fell over his broad forehead. Thick slabs of muscle covered his brawny, hairless chest. A tuft of black hairs sprouted from the top of his shorts and formed a thin trail to his navel. His skin was bronzed and shiny, and a couple of days' worth of beard growth outlined his square jaw. Jay looked just as good as I pulled off his T-shirt. Fine golden hairs swirled across his chest, his body lithe yet muscular. He wasn't as big as Tony, but his trim physique was tight and firm.

I moved toward Tony and plunged my tongue in his navel,

then worked it up his chest. He tasted salty, hot. By the time I got to his right pit and buried my nose in his stench, I was practically delirious, reeling in the splendor of his buff, sweaty bod. I looked over at Jay. He had one hand working his massive cock while the other kneaded his heavy, hairless balls.

With both hands I grabbed Tony by his drenched head and darted my tongue in his mouth. He tasted like cigarettes and 7Up. Our tongues wrestled for dominance as I dropped a hand to his crotch and squeezed his hard cock through his cotton shorts. Just then I felt a hot, sticky spray across my face. Tony and I pulled back from each other, our cheeks covered in Jay's frothy, salty jizz.

"Couldn't help it," Jay said, shrugging. "You're both so fuckin' hot."

Tony and I laughed hard. I was way past the whole officer/criminal fantasy. It was too much work, and besides, all I really wanted was my nine-inch cock up Tony's tight hole and Tony's pretty pink lips on Jay's awesome pecker. I'm a man of simple pleasures.

Jay moved close to me and licked his cum from my face, then did the same to Tony. As Tony's head dropped back in ecstasy under Jay's warm tongue bath, I pulled my cock out of my jeans and beat off. As soon as my boy had licked the stud's bronzed face clean, Tony dropped to his knees and engulfed Jay's semihard prick in his mouth. He sucked that pole like he'd mastered—maybe even taught—Cocksucking 101. There was no way he hadn't been with a guy before. Why'd I ever think he was straight?

Jay, whose own cum trickled from the corners of his mouth, moaned and leaned against the grimy stall wall as the hot construction worker licked my lover's bouncing sac, then took a hairy nut in his thick lips.

"Oh God," Jay groaned, as I got my cock good and hard to poke into Tony's ass. Tony wrapped his lips around the fat mushroom head of Jay's ten-inch prong. He grabbed Jay's taut asscheeks, and Jay drove his shaft in all the way to the base. Tony gagged a little, then adjusted his position and slurped back and forth on Jay's delicious, swollen meat.

My own cock was hard as concrete as I stroked myself, then plunged a finger into my puckered hole. I rocked back and forth, enjoying the sensation as much as I delighted in this nasty rest-stop show. The hot funk in the stall grew exponentially as Tony feasted on Jay's massive cock and I wildly finger-fucked my ass.

There wasn't much room in the stall, but I managed to pull Tony up so that his back was nearly horizontal to the floor. I reached into my jeans pocket and pulled out a condom. I tore open the wrapper with my teeth, then rolled the lubricated rubber onto my engorged pecker and pulled down Tony's soaking shorts and briefs. While Tony ran his mouth and tongue all over Jay's big cock, I spread his asscheeks wide and plugged Tony's hairy hole with my thumb. I twisted it left and right, then heard a sigh of pleasure squeak out of his cock-hungry lips.

"Hang on a sec," Jay said, then pulled the hunk's slobbering mouth off his prick. Jay hopped up on the toilet, his back against the wall. Flattening his back, Tony went back to his suckfest. I spread his beefy buttcheeks again, then ran the meaty tip of my cock along his furry, sweat-drenched crack.

"Errggh, ugggh," Jay groaned as he grabbed Tony's dark locks in both hands and face-fucked him. His expression twisted in pleasure as he blasted Tony's sloppy, sweat-drizzled lips with his power cock. I nudged my meat inside the stud's tight, slippery hole while Tony worked my boy into a frenzy that threatened to push him over the edge.

I went slow at first; like a vise I felt his ring clamp down on my tool then relax to suction more of me in. My meat was stone hard, the veins thick and near bursting. I grabbed Tony's hips and thrust inside him as he skillfully worked Jay's cock with his drooling mouth.

"Fuck yeah!" Tony cried out between slurps.

It must have been ninety-five degrees inside the restroom. Sweat dripped off Tony's forehead and landed in glistening pearls on Jay's pumping cock.

My own cock was plowing Tony's stretched hole. The muscles in his tight chute choked my meat, sending wave after wave of hot pleasure coursing through my body. I looked down to see Tony stroking his own meat hard and heavy, his powerful hand fisting his thick uncut cock.

I ran a hand up my soaked T-shirt, through the salt-and-pepper tufts on my well-toned chest, and ripples of hot man-musk wafted through the stall.

"Harder, Max, harder!" Tony cried out, as Jay's groans grew louder and louder.

"I'm gonna come. I'm gonna fucking come!" Jay called out.

"Yeah, I'm gonna shoot any second," I said, my bloated balls slapping against the back of Tony's furry nut sac.

"Fuck, yeah! Me too!" Tony groaned.

And then it happened. My entire body quaked as I shot a geyser of a cum load into Tony's hot ass. Jay quickly pulled out of Tony's mouth and gushed thick creamy cum all over the man's neck and chest. Then Tony stood, jerking and bucking, and sprayed his hot wad all over my weather-beaten mug.

I pulled off my T-shirt and cleaned off my face and Tony's. Jay and I kissed passionately as Tony stuck a couple of spit-drenched fingers up my ass and played with me for a while. I took Jay's big, spent cock in my hand and caressed it lovingly. "Good work, kid," I whispered in his ear. "Real good work."

The three of us cleaned up at the sinks and went out into the bright sun. I looked for Jay's Saturn but didn't see it. Tony's yellow pickup wasn't around either.

"How'd you guys get here?" I asked them.

"Greyhound," Jay said.

"So how you getting back?"

Tony smiled devilishly as he pointed to my rig. "Sleepover."

A couple of hours later I unloaded my eighteen-wheeler at a Chicago warehouse, where I ran into my old pal John, a brawny stud I knew from my days in Milwaukee. That night, the four of us got a motel room and fucked and sucked our brains out. It was the hottest ending imaginable to my twenty years on the road. And sweet, sexy Jay got to share every moment of my very last ride—this time in the flesh.

PRIZE BULL

Constantine Hiermaart

While I pissed in the restroom toilet, I read the notes scribbled on the stall walls. My cock hardened, and the flow of piss slowed, then dribbled to a stop.

My juicy man-pussy's wet and gagging. Anyone got a cucumber?

Free blow jobs. I live to suck cock.

I gently stroked my cock as it hardened.

Hugely hung trucker looking for nice juicy ass to pound. Fit, buff, horny with thirteen-inch rhino cock and big rhino balls aching to be drained.

I squeezed my cock and groaned as I read this one, imagining getting fucked up the ass by this trucker stud. I undid my belt buckle and top button and let my trousers fall to my knees. I rubbed my cock with my right hand then spat on my left middle finger. I slid it between my buttocks and rubbed around the hole, moaning. Imagining the trucker's big wet cock, I pushed my finger in and slid it back and forth, back and forth. I spread my legs and bent over as I finger-fucked myself, precum oozing from my cock and dripping to the floor. My open mouth was pressed against the stall wall, drooling saliva. The sweet moment came, and I spurted spunk to the floor with a splat.

I noted the trucker's email address on a sheet of toilet paper and got back to work with the mop, starting off by cleaning my cum off the floor. To most people the job of toilet attendant at the M63 Junction 4 rest area in Berkshire, UK, would have been the lowest job possible. For me it was like being in heaven. The smell of men: the pungent musky scent of their sweaty bodies and the stench of their cocks, balls, and asses. It was what I lived for. Every morning when I got to work, I sniffed that sexy smell in deep and imagined the beautiful beasts who had created it. I wasn't just a toilet attendant. I was a connoisseur!

Admittedly, not all the men who used the facilities were sexy, but plenty were, and over the course of a year my tastes had evolved from the traditional hunk to the truckers who frequently dropped by. I especially liked the big built ones, and believe me, some of them were built like bulls. I particularly liked the grimy and dirty guys, the ones who'd been on the road all night and were horny as fuck. The guys whose big cocks strained against their tight, sweaty jeans. I'd watch them by the urinal, big dirty fuckers, holding out their big wet swinging cocks, their piss sticky with precum.

The irony of all this was that despite being surrounded by these big swinging cocks, I'd never actually had any. It wasn't that I didn't want it. My ass was gagging for it. But in addition to being a connoisseur, I was a perfectionist. I didn't want my ass broken in by any old stray. I'd been watching the bull pen, waiting for the one. Waiting for the biggest and the best: the prize bull.

There was action in the M63 Junction 4 rest area toilets, for sure. I'd seen huge cocks poking out of jeans and listened to muffled grunts in the stalls. I'd spotted subtle signals and directions in the twitch of an eyebrow or the turn of a head. I even once looked through a small hole I'd made in a stall wall and watched a big trucker fuck a young man from the big city. My eyes were glued to the hole as the trucker grunted and groaned like a bull in heat, his big balls slapping against the young guy's thighs as he pounded his ass. *Mmmmmm.*

My manager, officious and bespectacled, had asked me to clean up the ubiquitous restroom graffiti, but I never had. I always told him I had cleaned the walls but they had been re-vandalized.

"What do we pay you for, boy?" he asked.

Sniffing around big dirty truckers? I thought.

I explained that I could hardly watch over men while they were in the stalls. He was a pushy little shit, and I resented him calling me "boy." Although I may have looked lithe and boyish, I was twenty-one, a grown man.

To my parents' dismay I had given up a place in college studying civil engineering to become the M63 Junction 4 rest area toilet attendant. I could hardly explain to them my passion, and when I visited them in the presence of their friends, they paid me to pretend that civil engineering was just the greatest thing and that I was going to graduate the following year.

Oh, if only they knew. I was going to graduate all right— with first-class honors, and I had just received my notification of final exam. I took the sheet of toilet paper and looked at the email address: rhino@fckmail.com. This nasty trucker would be the perfect teacher.

When I finished work at six P.M., I drove to the nearest town and found an Internet café. I ordered a cappuccino and sat down to write an email.

Hi, Rhinoceros. Juicy, wet, virgin man-pussy gagging for your big, wet rhinoceros cock. M63 Junction 4 rest area toilets. Time/date?

I pressed SEND and finished my coffee as I stared out the café window at a big shirtless workman drilling into the pavement. He was covered in sweat and glistened in the evening sun like a suburban Apollo. Truly magnificent.

I finished my coffee, licked the white froth from my lips, and was about to leave when an email suddenly appeared in my inbox.

I'm waiting for your pussy, boy. Noon tomorrow. You'll recognize me: I'm the biggest fuckin' trucker around.

When I arrived at work the next day I had brought along a big tube of lube, and I tried to decide on the best stall for my final exam. I eventually chose the handicapped stall for its size. My plan was to close the toilets for half an hour, pretending there was some kind of maintenance being done, and meanwhile the big guy could do his business on me.

At about 11:45 A.M. I started looking out for the guy. At 11:50 A.M. a trucker came in, but he was short and thin and could hardly be described as the "biggest fuckin' trucker around." At 11:55 A.M. an old man came in whistling some damn hymn and taking his time. In between mopping I scowled at him: I wanted the place empty.

After he left I got the CLOSED FOR MAINTENANCE sign ready and waited for Rhino. At dead-on noon, I heard a truck growling outside. With a big hiss it creaked to a stop and I waited, watching the door, my body in overdrive. A shadow appeared in the doorway and finally he entered. He hadn't exaggerated: He was muscular and stocky and deliciously dirty with long greasy hair, dirty stubble, and a cigarette hanging out of the side of his mouth. His jeans bulged obviously with his package, and as I stared he smiled. He was truly hung like a bull, and I surmised he must have been frequenting the place at night, because I would certainly have remembered him. I locked the door to the toilets and put up the CLOSED FOR MAINTENANCE sign.

The filthy trucker went to the urinal and then turned to me and winked. He undid his belt and zipper, and his cock swung out over the urinal, heavy and wet. It reached halfway to his knees, and I could see it pulsing slightly. With a grunt he started to urinate, and the piss descended with strings of sticky precum. Groaning slightly he massaged his cock and grinned.

I went to the door of the handicapped stall and winked at him as he had winked at me. Without zipping up his trousers, he turned from the urinal and walked to the stall, his tackle swinging. He entered, and I closed and locked the door behind us.

"You've seen my cock. Now I want to see your ass," Rhino said, his voice hoarse, deep, and horny.

"That seems fair," I told him.

"Bend over, boy," he growled.

With my back to him I pulled down my trousers.

"Bend over more."

I bent further, pushing my ass out for him.

"More," he said. "I wanna see your cute little ass."

I bent even further.

"That's good," he said with a grunt as he came up close behind me. He put some lube on his finger and slid it down to my asshole, then rubbed around it. I moaned loudly. With his other hand he massaged his huge cock as he grunted gently. He pushed his finger into my ass and started to finger-fuck me. "Is that good, boy?" he asked.

"Mmmm...more," I said.

He slid in another finger. "Is that good, boy?"

"Oh, yeah." I was grunting now.

He pushed in a third finger.

"Oh, man! Fuck me! Fuck me!" I shouted.

"Gotta make sure you can handle me, boy." The bull was now breathing heavily, and his cock was completely hard—thirteen inches of throbbing, thick, veiny cock. Glorious. Beautiful.

"You want some of this, boy?"

"Oh, God, yeah."

Grunting, the bull massaged his huge cock. Precum, sticky and wet, oozed down the huge shaft, its pungent stench filling the stall.

"I want to lick it up," I moaned.

"Okay. Lick me," he said, and turning around, I knelt in front of him.

I took his big wet cock in my hand. The stench was unbelievable, and it made me horny as fuck. I pulled back the foreskin and began by sucking the big head. He grunted loudly, his precum dribbling from the sides of my mouth as I sucked.

I reached down to his big balls and massaged them as he groaned. His grunting grew fast and heavy, and I knew it wouldn't be long. I didn't want him to come before I'd explored him properly, so I left his head and licked the length of his cock, then kissed and licked his big balls.

"Oh, yeah. You're good, boy," he said.

Rhino took off his jeans and spread his legs a little. I shoved my tongue and nose between his legs and licked around his big balls, sniffing his strong dirty musk in deep drafts. He was a prize bull, that was for sure, and I was going to taste his prize spunk.

I worked again on his cock, sucking his big head hard. His grunting again grew heavy and fast, but this time I kept going, working his cock with my tongue. I rubbed his big balls as he groaned, preparing them to be emptied.

"Oh, you're good, boy. You're damn good. Work that meat, boy," he said, caressing my head.

Finally, with the deep bellow of a bull in heat, he filled my mouth with hot spunk. He pumped his shaft, and more spurted over my face and into my mouth. I licked it up as he loudly moaned. After what seemed like a minute, his moans ceased and he sighed and sat heavily on the toilet seat, his cock swinging, spent and dripping.

I looked at it with disappointment. He lit a cigarette and took a few deep puffs. Then he looked at me as if reading my mind.

"Don't worry, boy. Your pussy'll get some. I'm a performer." He chuckled. "Let's take five."

Suddenly there was a shout from the front door of the toilets, and I panicked. The trucker put a finger to his mouth.

I unlocked the stall door and shut it behind me. Stepping out of the restroom, I found my manager, Mr. Montgomery. I could see from his face, cold as ice, that he had been there for quite some time.

"What, may I ask, is going on? 'Closed for maintenance'? What maintenance?" He sniffed the air and screwed up his face in disgust. "It smells like a cattle pen in there."

I had to think quickly, and in a flash my brain had it worked out. "Unfortunately, a disabled gentleman has had an accident," I said, whispering *accident* tactfully. "I've been helping him clear it up, but he is a *rather large* gentleman and it's quite hard work." I realized then that I was actually only telling one lie.

Mr. Montgomery's eyes narrowed. "Okay, I'll believe you this once. But if I find out there's been any funny business…"

"Oh, no, Mr. Montgomery. No funny business."

My boss crossed his arms. "You do realize that even though this job is about the lowest one possible, you can get sacked from it?"

"Yes, Mr. Montgomery."

"You do realize you only have this job because no one else will do it?"

"Yes, Mr. Montgomery."

"Very well. Get on with it then."

After I made sure he had gone out, gotten in his car, and driven away, I went back into the stall.

The bull was guffawing at me. "You're a clever boy, ain't you?" His dripping cock had grown heavy again, and as I locked the door I knelt down. I took his cock in my hand, pulled back the foreskin, and sucked. It throbbed, and the bull purred deeply.

"Show me your ass again, boy," he said. "That'll get me real horny!"

I turned my back to him and pulled down my trousers, pushing my ass as far as possible toward him. He knelt on the floor and pulled off my trousers. Then he kissed my ass and flicked his big tongue around my hole.

"What a nice juicy ass," he grunted. He spread my legs wide and sniffed and licked my balls and cock.

"Nice, young, juicy pussy," he moaned.

"Mmmmm."

The trucker sucked my cock and finger-fucked my ass while he rubbed his big, wet cock. Miraculously it was erect and throbbing again.

"We're back in business, boy," he said. "How do you want it?"

"Doggy," I told him.

I knelt on all fours and opened my ass for him, straining back and waiting for his cock, hot and wet, in my asshole. Although I wanted him in me real bad, I was also concerned I wouldn't be able to handle him. Looking over my shoulder, I watched as he heaved himself to his knees and got into position, massaging huge amounts of lube on his cock and quietly groaning. He rubbed his cock head around my asshole, and I moaned.

"Is that good, boy?"

"Mmmmm."

"You want some more?"

"Mmmmm."

With a deep grunt he pushed his head in, and I screamed as my ass opened. Even so, I wanted more and more.

"Fuck me deeper," I gasped.

He pushed deeper and deeper, grunting with each push until finally he was fucking me with his whole shaft.

"Fuck me. Fuck me, you big fuck. Fuck me until I can't take any more," I grunted.

He had begun by gently gliding his big cock in and out, but now he was gaining pace, pounding and pumping my ass, his big balls slapping against my thighs with each fuck.

"I'll fuck you good, boy," he grunted. "I'll fuck you real good."

Just when I thought I'd burst and come all over the floor, he stopped.

"Why don't we try a different position, boy?" he said.

He heaved himself from the floor and sat on the edge of the toilet seat, his legs wide apart. I looked with wonder at his huge tree trunk of a cock and his gigantic balls hanging like ripe, juicy plums.

I sat astride him and put my tongue in his mouth. I smelled this dirty man and groped his powerful shoulders and chest. He caressed my whole body with his rough hands, then grabbed my buttocks and squeezed them. He found my ass again with his fingers and took his big wet cock and rubbed it up and down my ass crack. Our tongues entwined and I pushed down on his cock, wanking him with my buttocks. Then I grabbed his cock and pushed it into my ass.

I pumped his cock with my ass as he grunted louder and louder, grinding his teeth and roughly massaging my buttocks.

"Pump it, boy. Pump it hard. Pump it good."

I worked his cock with my ass, squeezing and pumping until he was snarling and bellowing. I worked him until he was on the edge of orgasm, until he was nearly bursting. As I slowed and pulled his cock down I brought him back from the edge. I pumped him hard again, bringing him to the edge again, only to bring him down again. I prolonged this for a few minutes until he groaned and moaned in agony and pleasure.

"Oh, God...God...God," the trucker cried, squeezing my buttocks hard. "Please...please...please."

Finally I put him out of his misery and brought him to climax, pumping him fast and hard. He bellowed like a big fucking bull in heat as he finally filled me with his hot spunk. It spilled out from the sides of my ass, which were sore from fucking, and down to his fat balls. At the same time, I exploded, spraying cum all over his face. When he finally was empty he licked my spunk from his lips and grinned at me, exhausted.

It had been done. I was no longer a virgin. The prize bull had the honor of breaking in my ass, which, fucked and sore, throbbed with gratitude. I watched him as he rested on the toilet seat, gasping. He was magnificent.

Although I continued to enjoy truckers, I eventually decided to go back to college. I studied civil engineering, and three years later I graduated with first-class honors. I now work as a town planner and have settled down with a man. He may not be a prize bull, but he's mine and I love him. We have a mortgage and a steady, stable life, with dinner parties, holidays in Tuscany, and snuggles by the fireplace.

Although my days of exploration in the M63 Junction 4 rest area toilets are well and truly over, whenever I pass by and go in for a piss, I sniff deeply and remember the prize bull and those thirty minutes of hot, ass-pumping excitement.

RASSLIN' RED

Bearmuffin

I was feeling mean, horny, and downright fucking funky as my '55 Ford pickup kicked up a trail of dust down the long, lonesome highway. It had been one hell of a day. I'd just put in ten hours of backbreaking work, and it was hotter than Hades, so I peeled off my grimy, sweat-stinking T-shirt.

I had one hand on the wheel, the other gliding along my hairy pecs and sweaty abs. My horny cock was swelling up, growing raging hard as I thought of my good buddies back at the construction site with their shirts off.

I fuckin' loved the way their tight, worn jeans hugged their bulging crotches and beefy butts. Yes, sir! They were a wild herd of sexy, hardworking studs all right. I got hornier than hell thinking about their lean, muscled, macho bods dripping with hot, funky sweat as they worked under the blazing sun.

I had to pop a few buttons off my jeans and give my squirming wanger some breathing room. Thick, salty drops of precum oozed and frothed out of my gaping-wide pee hole. I grabbed my jizzing joint, gave it a few hearty whacks, and felt a gusher of a spurting load about to come on when from out of nowhere I saw this giant figure of a trucker-fucker standing by his rig with a flat tire.

I pulled over and asked the stranger if he needed help. The stud aimed a swift kick at the blown-out tire with his boot, snarled a curse, and climbed into my pickup. A strange self-satisfied smirk was plastered on his kisser.

"Thanks for the lift," he said. He grabbed my hand and almost pulverized it with a bone-crushing shake. Come to think of it, the bare-chested stud was as broad and brawny as one of those TV wrestlers. He had his sweaty T-shirt tucked under a thick rawhide belt that circled his powerful waist. He told me his name was Red. It was easy to see how he got his name.

Thick swirls of copper-red hair swarmed every inch of his burly, muscle-packed torso. A long shaggy mane of dark red hair framed his powerful square-jawed face. The thick, coppery hairs sprouting from his cleft cheeks and circling around his thick, full lips lent the aggressive trucker an even more macho, grizzly-bear look.

"My buddy Hank has a filling station about fifteen miles down the road," he said. "You'd be doing me a big favor if you'd drop me off. That is, if you don't mind."

"Sure, pal," I told him. "No problem." Hell, this was one hot bruiser you just couldn't say no to. Not with those smoldering, deep-set green eyes that flashed like emeralds in a bonfire.

Red's craggy face was flushed like he was worked up about something. But the dizzying macho stench floating from his sopping-wet, hairy armpits was getting me more than a little excited, too.

When Red shot a lingering glance at my hard, quivering cock

jutting between my splayed legs, a broad wolfish grin broke out on his face. He reached toward my sweating pecs to give one of my thick, protruding nipples a hearty tweak. My foot slipped on the gas pedal, and I damn near ran us right off the fuckin' road.

"Whoa, good buddy!" I said, pulling off to the side of the road. "Ya want something to work on? Well, suck my dick!"

Red sure as hell wasn't waiting for an engraved invitation. The trucker-fucker dove between my thighs and wrapped his hot, horny, and bearded lips around my cock. The stud took all ten inches of my throbbing, precum-drooling cock down his throat in one feisty gulp.

Hot fuckin' damn! While the horny trucker sucked my crank, I reached for his bulging crotch to pop open the buttons on his dusty 501s. Out sprouted eleven inches of thick, veiny, uncut cock-meat. I grabbed Red's spasming, expanding cock and felt those thickly corded, pulsing veins burn into my hand. I made a fist around his raging hard-on and gave it a big squeeze.

Red gurgled hungrily as he slobbered over my precum-dripping bull-meat. I slipped my hand over his fat dick. Sliding his raunchy foreskin all the way back to his sweat-soaked, musk-stinking pubes, I exposed the wide cock head that slowly oozed thick salty drops of sputtering pre-jizz.

"Ya got one hell of a hot, stinking jizz-stick there, buddy!" Red moaned huskily. The stud's thick, drooling tongue shot from his slobbering lips. He hungrily ran his licker up and down my sweaty fuck-pole, lapping up the thick drops of precum oozing from my piss hole.

"Damn! Yeah, fucker! Suck my dick!" I was howling like a wild dog. I grabbed his shaggy red mane and forced his hot mouth over my raging cock. My cum-churning nuts spread over his chin as I thrust my sweaty groin in his face, forcing my dick all the way down his cocksucking throat.

I moaned and squirmed, bucked my hot ass over the seat. Red took the opportunity to work a hand under my fat balls. His thick, wiggling finger split my sweaty buns apart and poked into my asshole. Then it lunged inside me, boring into my ass like a power drill.

The fucker had me going out of my mind. "AWWWW, FUCK!" I yowled. "UNNGH, UNNGH, UNNGH!! I'M GONNA SHOOT!" Red sucked my spasming cock as he finger-fucked my hot ass in a wild frenzy. The cocksucking pleasure flashed from my cum-scorched balls up through my body until it boggled my fuckin' mind.

"SUCK IT, STUD! SUCK IT! AWWWWW!" I hollered like a wild man as Red clamped his burning lips down hard around my jizzing dick. "FUCK!!!" I shot, shot, and fuckin' shot thick spurts of hot spunk into his gurgling, sopping-wet mouth.

"Fuck, yeah!" Red groaned thickly. He clenched his rough hands around my hot nuts, squeezing the fuckin' cum out of them. My jizz-slippery cock slipped from his mouth and slapped him square in the face. It waved back and forth like a fireman's hose gone out of control, drenching him with hot, thick spurts of fuck-jizz that dribbled over his bearded jowls and chin.

All I had to do now was give Red's mighty trucker whanger a good squeeze to send the fucker gasping and spasming in dazed ecstasy.

"AWWWWW! FUUUUCK YEEAAAH!" Red rocked back and forth as his cock exploded in my fist. Big hot fuck-wads sprayed from his wide, gaping piss-slit and vaulted high in the air. They splattered all over my windshield and dashboard, drenching us two horny fuckers in an ocean of hot, sizzling man-fuck!

"HOLY SHIT!" I exclaimed. Using my shirt, I mopped the

cum off my face. "I'm sweating like a fuckin' pig!" I said.

"Fuck!" Red sported a shit-eatin' grin. "I could use a shower myself." He pointed to a dirt road. "If ya just go down here and make a left, we'll be at Hank's in no time at all."

We pulled onto a broad stretch of dirt and gravel shaded by towering oak trees. A shack—surrounded by big rigs, Harley-Davidsons, and pickup trucks—stood between a gasoline pump and an outhouse. We heard loud cries and lusty shouts from inside the shack. Hell, it sounded like a fuckin' riot was going on!

"C'mon!" Red pushed me through the door. "Hank must be partying with his buddies!"

It took a minute for my eyes to adjust to the almost pitch-black darkness. I couldn't believe my eyes. What the hell was going on? The place was jam-packed with sweating, stinking truckers and bikers. Some of them were toking on thick stogies, but everybody was swilling down whiskey and cold beer out of glass jars. The guys were howling at the tops of their lusty lungs as they whacked off their hot man-tools.

They cheered and jeered as two buck-naked burly studs grappled on top of a battered, cum-soaked mattress. The two funky men were at it hammer and tongs. Hot steaming sweat slid off their straining muscles as they wrestled in the harsh light cast by a naked bulb swinging from the rafters on a frayed three-foot-long cord.

"Go on, Bruno, ya faggot!" the bikers screamed. "Kick his ass!"

Bruno was a dark, monster-muscled biker. His name was tattooed over his wide, hairy chest in large gothic letters. He had long black hair and deep-set black eyes that glittered with a macho, almost evil, intensity. His powerful square jaw and chin were covered with thick, blue-black beard stubble. Fuck! Bruno was one hell of a very scary but very sexy stud.

Bruno's thick, rippling muscles were bulging around Jake. Jake was a giant bulldozer of a trucker with broad shoulders, tree-trunk thighs, and thick pumped pecs that glistened with a fine sheen of manly sweat. "C'mon, Jake!" the truckers hollered at him. "Fuck him! Fuck that stinkin' biker!"

Jake's strong, craggy face grimaced in pain and lust. His baby-blue eyes were burning into Bruno's masterful glare. Jake's golden-blond hair was cropped just an inch above the scalp of his bullet-shaped head. His thickly veined, uncut cock jabbed deeply into Bruno's hairy, furrowed abs.

Bruno's precum-dripping monster dong sliced under Jake's low-swinging, sweat-drenched bull-nuts. The muscles of both muscle-bound studs strained to the max as each tried to topple the other to the ground.

A thick haze of blue-gray smoke floated over the sweating crowd of naked, lusty men. Ten- and twenty-dollar bills were tossed into a trucker's red Peterbilt cap as the men betted on their favorite stud to win the wrestling match.

Red and I squeezed our way through the sardine-packed crowd. Horny, anxious hands came out of nowhere, pawing at my pecs and pinching my nipples. Within seconds our jeans had been ripped off. A big tattooed biker stuck his hairy hand up my ass. He was ready to finger-fuck me, but Red whacked the horny stud, sending him reeling to the ground.

"YEAH! YEAH! YEAH!!" A mighty, thundering roar went up among the studs. Bruno had twisted one of Jake's huge, muscular arms behind his back. He flung the blond trucker onto the stinking, cum-splattered mattress. In a flash the victorious biker scrambled over Jake, pinning the stud between his hairy, sweaty thighs.

The raunchy, sweat-soaked men were howling wildly. They

jumped up and down like angry gorillas as they worked their sweaty fists over their lust-bloated tools in a fuck-mad frenzy. "Fuck him, Bruno!" they screamed. "FUCK HIM!!!"

With a lusty shout, Bruno squatted over Jake's upturned face to smother the blond trucker with his beefy, stinking ass. Jake gasped for air. He struggled and squirmed on the mattress. Bruno gloated with triumph.

"Yeah, fuck face! Eat my fuckin' ass. Eat it!"

Bruno ground his hairy butt over Jake's hunching face. The blond stud's cock quivered then bolted upright as thick precum oozed from his fat piss-slit, slowly dripping over his fuzzy, cum-churning bull-nuts.

Jake sucked in his cheeks as his hot tongue popped out of his slobbering mouth to wiggle up Bruno's funky butthole. The blond trucker's muscular body shuddered with lust, his thick thighs spread wide apart. His fat, sweaty nuts bounced up and down as his thick trucker dong spasmed while he rimmed Bruno's dark puckered asshole.

"Yeah, unnngh. Fuck, yeah. Eat my ass! Eat it good!"

Bruno bucked and squirmed, firmly impaled on Jake's lunging licker. Jake grabbed Bruno's slimy buttcheeks and split them apart to drive his drilling tongue all the way up the furry biker's hole.

Bruno flung his mighty head back, arching backward as he fisted his steaming fuck-tool. Rivers of hot sweat poured over his bulging, shuddering muscles. "Unngh, unngh. UNNNNGH, YOW!!!" Bruno's thick bull-cock expanded and jerked, then finally exploded. Thick wads of fizzing trucker jizz blasted from his swinging bull-nuts through his cock and out his spurting piss-slit.

"NNYYAARGH!" Jake bellowed as he shot spurt after fuck-raging spurt of thick fuck-wads. The hot sperm flashed through the air and mixed with Bruno's burning shower of man-jizz.

"FUCK! FUCK!! FUCK!!!" Bruno screamed hoarsely. His hot man-cock went off like a Roman candle, spasming wildly over and over as it sprayed hot stinking jets of milky semen over the throng of lusty, sweaty truckers and bikers. They roared and screamed as they shot their heavy fuck-loads. Huge, hearty gobs of hot spunk blasted from their heavy, low-hanging balls. The hot jizz arced right into the air, splashing down hard on us until every stinking, sweating stud in the shack was smeared and dripping wet with thick, slimy streams of man-fuck.

"YEAH!" howled a self-satisfied Bruno as he climbed off Jake's ass-sucking face. The victorious stud picked up the cap full of money and joined the rest of his biker buddies.

"Shee-it! There ya are, ya ol' son of a bitch!" a sweaty and cum-soaked trucker cried, slapping Red on the back and shooting me a mean and nasty glare full of lust.

"This here's Hank," Red said.

"Me and the guys were wondering if you two studs were up to putting on a little rasslin' show for us," Hank said.

Red's eyes lit up and a wolfish grin spread across his roguish face. "How 'bout it?" He grabbed my thick, horny nipples and gave them a hearty tweak.

"Well, I dunno, guys," I said. Fuck! The very idea of wrestling with Red in front of all these horny maniacs turned me on, but it had me pissing in my pants, too. "Maybe."

The men listening in on the conversation growled impatiently, their horny faces flushed hot with anger and excitement. The stinking, sweating studs surrounded us, jacking their cocks.

"Take your pick, stud!" Red hooted. "You can either rassle me or take on every last sweatin', stinkin' guy in the place!"

Red, Hank, and the rest had me cornered now. I felt the wild, macho heat burning inside their bodies, cocks, and balls. No, siree! These studs weren't going to take kindly to a no from me. I had to agree.

"Okay, studs," Red growled, slapping my sweaty, meaty ass. "But remember," he hissed, winking at them broadly, "his ass is mine!"

The sweaty crowd broke out laughing. The studs crowded around the cum-stained mattress. As Red and I began wrestling, the men howled at us. Thick, lusty drops of precum sputtered from their thick, veiny dicks.

I tried to outmaneuver the mighty Red, but the stud was lightning quick. He lunged at me, catching me fast in a face-crushing headlock.

Red mashed my sweaty face into his raunchy, man-stinking armpit. The powerful wet, musky stink rushed up my nose. It turned me on, making my dick quiver and shake. My cum-bloated balls bounced around my low-swinging nut sac.

"Yeah, ya fucker!" Red hissed. "Ya like that fuckin' man-stink dontcha? So lap it up, stud! Lick my pits!"

My stinking licker came flying out of my mouth. I swirled it along Red's musky, sweat-dripping armpit hairs. The hairs scratched my face and wrapped around my flickering tongue. Potent blasts of hot, pungent man-stench scorched my tongue. Red's funky stink rushed up my wide-open nostrils, sending hot tears streaming down my sweaty, suffocating face.

Red held me fast in a powerful belly-to-belly bear hug. Our cocks sputtered hard and long, thrusting upward, trapped between our sweat-drenched, hard-muscled abs. Precum drooled from our slits, flowing in one long, sputtering drizzle onto the mattress.

The red-maned trucker forced his slobbering tongue between my lips and mashed his lusty thick licker against mine. The fierce stud grunted and groaned, eagerly swapping hot macho spit with me until it frothed and bubbled down the corners of our gaping, gasping mouths.

I bucked but to no avail. Fisting their stinking, dripping cocks, the studs roared with delight at my predicament. I yelped and squirmed, but I was trapped in Red's powerful grip. The stud dug his thick, hairy fingers into my sweating haunches. He twisted and slapped my hot, slimy stud-melons, then peeled my buns wide apart with his thick trucker thumbs.

"YEEAHH!" Red howled fiercely. His savage face was contorted with macho lust. "Gonna fuck ya, stud!" he growled. "Gonna fill your hot stinkin' stud ass full of bull-cock." He hoisted me on top of his fat, sputtering rod.

"NNNOOO! AWWWW! GODDAMNNN! FUUUUCK!" I screamed as the burly stud rammed his fiery bull-meat all the fucking way up my ass. The truckers and bikers raised holy hell. They screamed and howled like banshees as Red man-fucked the living daylights out of me.

I wrapped my legs around Red's waist, and my burly arms flew around his thick, vein-corded bull-neck as he brutally slammed into me. The fucker chewed on my sweat-soaked nipples, slobbering over my huge slabs of hard, hot muscle. My eyes rolled back in my sockets, and my drooling tongue flopped out of my mouth as my cock-hungry butthole sucked around Red's plowing pile-driver fuck-meat. "AAAAH, FUCK ME! FUCK ME, STUD!" I howled.

Some of the men were already shooting off their thick loads. Their piss-slits opened wide, and out flew thick, stinking blasts of jizz that splattered on our bodies and drenched our lust-tangled bods.

"Yeah, stud," Red grunted. "UNNNGH, UNNNGH, UNNNGH! I'm fuckin' your ass, good buddy. I'm fuckin' your stinking ass but good!" Red's boulderlike muscles rippled and bulged as his hairy butt heaved and bucked back and forth. The stud slammed his thick eleven-inch trucker's tool in and out of my funk-dripping butthole. His mouth yawned open. "AW-WWW FUCK! AWWW JEEEZ!" he cried. "GONNA SHOOT! GONNA FUCKIN' SHOOT!"

His blazing eyes bulged, and his hot mouth dropped wide open. His slobbering tongue flopped out of his drooling mouth as he power-slammed his dick of death up my burning, aching butthole.

"AAAAAAAAAARGH!!!" Red slammed forward one last time. He buried his bull-joint to the root as his hairy, swinging balls smashed against mine. Big scalding cum spurts pumped up my jizz-scorched hole. The burning cum sprayed from his stud-nuts, filling my ass with hot trucker spunk. I squirmed and heaved, my hot asshole squeezing around the thick root of his cock to suction every last drop of hot cum from his fat balls.

"UNNNGH! UNNNGH! AWWWW FUCK! GODDAMN FUUCCCKKK!" I screamed. My cock swelled up and exploded. Thick jets of semen hurtled between our jizz-soaked bodies. The cum spumed out like a fuckin' geyser, spraying hot man-fuck everywhere. The men roared and screamed, shooting their heavy pent-up fuck-wads until every last stinking trucker and biker had emptied his hairy nuts and was drenched in a stinking, gushing sea of cum.

The studs were hot for my sweet, juicy ass now! Wild, lusty grins broke out across their faces. Their bloated cocks quivered, and their feisty, cum-swollen balls rumbled as they came toward me.

I lay sprawled on the spunk-soaked mattress, drenched in an ocean of sweaty man-fuck. A few studs scrambled over me, pawing my ass, grabbing my balls. But several others pushed them back. One by one the studs came up and formed a line. Anxiously they fisted their cocks, waiting for their turn to plug my aching butthole and cock-thirsty mouth.

I turned my head to see Red standing at the end of the line with a crazed, shit-eating grin plastered on his craggy trucker's kisser. The red-haired brute pumped his thick, pulsing-veined cock. It shook and quivered. His hot balls bobbed up and down in his furry nut sac as thick precum drops fizzled from his huge piss-slit and slithered to the ground in a huge cum puddle between his hairy toes.

"Hey, Red!" I hollered. "What the fuck are ya waitin' for?"

The trucker broke out in a wild laugh that shook the rafters. "Just savin' the best for last, stud!"

HORSE SENSE

Rob Kilmer

I'd never woken up with my head in a horse's feed bucket before, but then again I'd never had a night like that one in Alabama.

I was making an Ocala run, heading down to Pershing Farms with two mares and a foal. The boss down there, Michael Malloy, is one of the few who doesn't subcontract out his trucking, so he keeps three of us drivers on staff to haul his horses to the racetracks and other farms. Michael and I had a thing when we were in our early twenties. It lasted about a year, but he got tired of me being on the road twenty-five days of the month. And hell, I was a horny kid back then and didn't see any harm in popping what I could on the road. It had nothin' to do with Michael being at home, waiting for me.

Ah, well, I can't lie. They don't call me Robby the Knob for my good looks.

That Wednesday morning, I loaded up at Rockaround

Farms, one of those "boutique" horse operations that are so fancy you're nervous to spit on the ground. There were orange traffic cones set up a half-mile from the loading area. A groom ran out waving his arms and made me park way out from the barn.

"What the hell's going on?" I asked Mitch, the head groom, after that hike up the drive.

"Mrs. Pelland has decided she wants a goddamned burgundy-and-yellow color scheme," he answered in between chews on his toothpick. "So, guess what? She's getting a goddamned burgundy-and-yellow color scheme."

"In a horse barn?" I said.

"And we get to move all the horses out, repaint every stall on the property, then move the horses back in."

"Maybe she'll want you to dye the horses burgundy, too."

Rodney smiled. "Maybe I'd dye them yellow. It'd be a helluva surprise to see palomino horses show up to run the Kentucky Derby."

Horse operations have a weird mix of people in them. You got your owners who are so rich I swear they have someone else wipe their butts. You got your barn managers who are frazzled as shit trying to keep the owners, the staff and the horses happy. There's the grooms and barn help who actually do the scut work, and there's the occasional walker. Walkers are what we call those guys (they're almost always guys), who hitchhike the circuit, picking up cash at one barn or another and crashing in a spare horse stall.

We watched the grooms do a final brush-out of the two mares I was picking up. The one mare's little foal jittered around, tugging at its purple halter, antsy.

"You got the big rig today. More pickups to do on the way back?" Mitch asked.

"Naw, just these two. I dropped off eight horses over to Aiken."

"Cold front coming down."

"I think I'll outrun it. Stay on 65 all the way."

"Nice drive."

The horses and their—no shit—bottled water got loaded, and we said our good-byes.

I'd let the mares load after checking their lip tattoos. I learned that lesson early. Once, I grabbed a bay stallion that the farm grooms led out to me—and shoot, what a pisser he was to load and unload, 1,200 pounds of hormone-addled fuckhead-edness—drove him 1,800 miles back home and then Michael told me I'd brought the wrong damn horse. Felt like an idiot. Thoroughbreds look an awful lot alike, especially the bays, so now instead of trusting the grooms to bring me the right horse, I always check their lips before I let 'em load. And foals'll only follow their mamas the first few months anyway, so I wasn't worried about the baby.

I-65 cuts through West Kentucky, a hilly, gorgeous part of the state where the grass really does have a blue tinge to it, something to do with the nitrogen content or something. My CD player cranked out Green Day and Lighthouse and just for old time's sake, a little Aerosmith. Good driving music.

I saw the kid the first time at a rest stop just past the Alabama state line. Four hours into the trip and it was time to feed and water the horses and take a piss myself. I'm sometimes tempted to just unzip in the trailer and let the hay on the floor suck it up, but unless there's snow to slog through, I go into the men's room. Interesting places sometimes, men's rooms, especially after midnight, if you know what I mean.

Anyway, this kid was going from rig to rig, his shaggy blond hair blowing in the breeze. He was slender, maybe five-six, and looked to be about a buck twenty. Jockey wannabe? He was wearing a denim jacket with a big hole on the left arm, torn, like someone tried to rip the jacket off him. His jeans were scruffy and matched his dirty backpack.

A walker, I decided. Or a hustler maybe, trading blow jobs for cash.

He was at the rig next to me, talking to the driver, the breeze carrying over bits of their conversation. Something along the lines of "How far you going?" and "Miami," and "Can you help unload in Orlando?"

Now that he was closer, I could see the kid was early twenties, maybe. Okay, technically not a kid, but a kid to me. Turning thirty-five in March had bothered me a lot more than turning thirty had—weird but true. Not that I'd fallen to pieces, but I sure felt the long days now: my legs and back stiff as hell climbing down from the rig after a trip, headaches if I drove into the sun too long, my legs and feet aching most nights.

Looking this guy over on this breezy March morning made me ache somewhere else, though. He was fair-skinned, not so white as to be sickly looking—just creamy, with freckles on his face. Made me think he hadn't been on the road too long. I was hoping the other trucker would turn him down and he'd head my way, but to my disappointment, he and the other driver shook hands through the driver's window and the kid trotted around the front of the truck. The truck bellowed out a cloud of smoke, ground its gears, and Blond Boy was carried away, out of my life forever.

Or so I thought.

Once I got to Montgomery, I had to make the call to take it all the way through, which was another six hours, or bed down

just past Dothan. There's an equine motel there that lets you put
your horses in a corral for the night and let them stretch their
legs. I always carry our own hay, of course, and for this group,
that bottled water. Ten of those five-gallon jugs—said jugs of
which I declined to load myself, thank you very much.

I took the exit onto State Road 231, aiming to have dinner at
the steakhouse in Ozark. They've got a truckers' parking lot in
the back, and they're pretty good about seating us where we can
watch our rigs. Plus, I think they kinda want to keep us truckers
away from the workaday clientele. Can't say I blame 'em.

I pulled in next to another horse rig I recognized. The wind
had picked up, and it blew some hay strands around when I
gave the girls a snack and fresh bottled water. I locked up. Once
inside the restaurant I spotted old Henry Clayburn, another
horse trucker. We shared the booth and shot the shit, having as
much good talk and fun as you can have without liquor being
involved. I'm straight up when it comes to taking care of the
horses. You can't take chances with this level of animal.

I felt good after dinner, a little drowsy with my stomach full.
Four-thirty. I slept for a while in Dothan, and after another
glance at the mares, I hit the road again.

Several hours later, I took the right jog off of 1 and headed
west on a dirt road. A drizzle started to mist up the night, so
I flicked on the wipers. The mares were kicking around in
the trailer, moving in the narrow stalls. I felt the shift of their
weight.

They must've known it was bedtime. I could tell they were
antsy and wanted to stretch.

Some nights the motel is self-serve. Clyde, the owner, shows
horses of his own, and when he's off the property us regulars
open the front gate with our own key and grab room keys
from beneath his mailbox. Three trailers are the rooms for the

humans, and he has ten acres of pasture space for the horses. I
snagged a key.

The rain splatted cold on my face and hands when I got
out of the rig. The security lights flipped on, and a bat zipped
around them. The wind was blowing steady from the north,
chilly enough to make me wish I'd brought my down vest. The
mares snorted in the trailer, restless. One of them kicked out,
and the wall vibrated, a cold, metallic sound. Then I heard a
thump from inside—a weird thump, though—it didn't sound
horsey to me.

Maybe one of those damned water bottles had fallen over.

I opened the first stall door and saw a flash of blue off to my
left. A handful of hay was pressed against my face. I felt fingers
against my shirt, hands pushing me out of the way, and I hun-
kered down, my arms out, and grabbed at whatever I could get
hold of. My eyes were watering from the hay dust, so I couldn't
see too well, but I sure could feel—a small guy, smacking his
fists against my neck and head, gasping, then kicking against my
shins as I lifted him up and threw him against the back wall of
the trailer. He let out an *oomph* of pain then slid down the wall,
his jacket scooching up over him like blue wings.

The kid from back at the rest stop.

Bessie, the mare, was skittering all over the stall, jerking her
head, snorting. I kept one eye on the kid, who was still on his
ass in the hay, and spoke low and soft to the mare. "Hey, hey,
Bessie baby, hey girlie, it's all right." I took a few deep breaths,
letting my adrenaline notch back, knowing she could smell it if
I was wired up. I made my voice low and quiet, all calm-like:
*Everything's fine. It's perfectly normal to have some stranger in
your stall. It's okay, little lady.* Her ears rotated back and forth,
from me to the kid, and after a minute or so she settled down. I
gave her an apple from her treat bag.

When I turned back to the kid, he was shaking his head and rubbing his face, looking real groggy.

And bloody.

Oh, shit, I didn't hit him that hard, did I?

Maybe I had.

I flipped on the overhead light and squatted in front of the door. And waited.

The kid opened his eyes and elbowed up, leaning on one side. He wiped one hand over his scalp, and it came away red and wet. He looked puzzled.

"Who the hell are you and what are you doing with my horses?" I said.

"I just wanted someplace warm to sleep, dude." His voice sounded threadbare, as worn as his jeans.

"Did you do anything to them?"

"What?"

"The horses! Did you touch them? Give them anything?"

"No, man. I don't know shit about horses. Honest." He raised his palms to me. "I just needed to…" He swallowed and looked away from me. His left eye was a little swollen, his bottom lip cut and bleeding.

"Needed to what?"

"Get away from the trucker I was with. He was looking for rough trade and that's not my deal."

"What is your deal?"

"My deal is I'm trying to get down to Tampa, and I do what I have to."

"What's in Tampa?"

"My aunt and cousins. They're gonna help me get a job at the stadium."

I looked at him more closely and could tell he'd been smacked around by life in general. I saw his knobby collarbone under his shirt. His hands were slender and worn. He was thin—not the kind of thin that's fashionable and lean, the kind of thin that says, *I haven't been eatin' regular.* Probably grew up in the Midwest, quit high school, then knocked around—and got knocked around himself ever since. These kinds of guys are the walkers, moving from one place to another, never staying long.

Could have been me fifteen years ago. Except that I'd found the farm, and eventually Michael found me.

I held out one hand. "Come on."

The kid's eyes narrowed as he stood up. "So what's your deal?"

"I'm gonna get these horses settled in for the night. You can either clean up inside"—I jerked my chin toward the trailers—"or hit the road. Your choice."

I was hoping he'd stay.

He gazed up at me for a long time. His eyes were pale blue, almost eerie looking in the moon light. He took the key from me, careful not to touch my hand. "I'm Sean."

"Robert."

"Thanks, Robert. Really. Thanks."

A half-hour later, I had the mares unloaded, brushed out, and fed. The three-month-old foal flitted around the paddock, clumsy. His long legs weren't wired a hundred percent yet. He stumbled once, fell down on his face, then popped back up with a *Who the hell just pushed me?* expression. I couldn't help laughing out loud.

"What's so funny?" It was Sean's voice, sounding stronger.

"Foals always crack my shit up." As if to prove my point, the foal leapt straight into the air, kicked out with his rear legs, then took off at a run.

Sean smiled. "He's cute as shit."

"They're all cute. Even the ugly ones."

"How can a horse be ugly? They always look beautiful to me."

"You work horses?"

"Naw," he said. "I grew up in Detroit."

Sean stood next to me, and the clean scent of Dial soap hit my nose. His clean hair was wet and slicked back.

"Let me see these," I said, and motioned to the cuts on his face.

When he turned to me, those pale eyes hit me again and made my belly tighten. Who wouldn't want a blond boy like this?

The cut over his left eye wasn't too bad, and his lip had stopped bleeding. Still, it was a little puffy and tender looking. I was tempted to bend down and kiss it, but I didn't.

"You hurt anyplace else?" I asked him.

"No, I got away before the guy could get too worked up."

"You'll live. In the meantime, you wanna find out more about horses?"

"Sure," he said, his eyes brightening.

I handed him two carrots. Both of the mares smelled it, snorted, and ambled over to the fence. Sean leaned back as they put their chests against the fence and reached out, mouths open, teeth exposed.

"Whoa!" he exclaimed.

"Break those in half and put them crossways, not lengthwise. Put your palm flat out so they don't grab a finger or two."

"You sure they won't bite?"

"You never know."

He glanced up at me, saw I was teasing, then relaxed. "Here ya go, ladies."

The mares snuffled over his hands and took the carrots delicately. Silver Star moved away once she realized Sean didn't have any more treats, but Bessie stayed, sniffing Sean's hands and jacket.

"She's friendly, for a thoroughbred," I said.

"These are racehorses?"

"Not anymore. They're broodmares. But yeah, they both raced."

Sean had stopped listening, I could tell. He ran his hands over Bessie's muzzle, smiling when she put her forehead against his chest. His slender fingers stroked her long ears. "She's great!"

"Now that you got to know the front end, want to help with the back end?"

"I guess."

"Come on. I need to get the stalls mucked out."

Sean worked hard, scooping out the wet hay and shit, hustling the wheelbarrow down to the manure pile. Within twenty minutes, we had those two stalls spic and span. Dust from the fresh hay hung in the air, and Sean sneezed three times then laughed.

He made me laugh, too, and in that moment I fell for him— just a little.

When he saw me looking at him, his smile changed from something fun loving and innocent to something stirring and not so innocent. He leaned back against the two hay bales, arms out, legs apart.

My cock snaked up in my shorts and began to pay attention.

Sean shrugged off his jacket. "I'm a little warm."

"You're a little hot," I told him.

His shirt came off next. His chest was slender, smooth, tightly muscled. Not from weight lifting. It looked like he really worked for a living. A sexy tendril of fuzz started just below his belly button.

By the time I took the five steps over to him, his boots and pants were off. His briefs were gray, and the tantalizing tip of his pale cock peeked out at the top. He was a real blond, judging from his tufts of reddish-gold pubic hair. His legs were solid and evenly muscled.

His lips trembled as I stepped closer. "Wanna fuck?" he said flatly.

"Love to." I met his eerie gaze, those pale eyes on me like lasers.

He didn't glance away. A little smile turned up the edges of his mouth. Quick as a snapping turtle, he grabbed my neck and pulled me close. His lips were against mine, then his tongue, probing at my mouth. I groaned and melted against him.

He sat up, his long, pink cock banging against his belly.

"Nice," I commented.

"Are you gonna give me a hand?"

"I'll give you more than a hand." I reached into Bessie's water bucket and splashed him, using my hands to smooth the water off that beautiful skin, watching his shivers as the cold water hit him in all the warm places. I shucked his shorts the rest of the way down. His pink nipples felt just right in my teeth; I sucked and nipped, and he gave a laughing moan from deep in his chest.

I grabbed his cock. It was pink and firm, bouncing as I wrapped my palm around him. The water made him slippery, and I lost my grip a couple of times as I jerked him off. He leaned against the hay, the water trickling down his torso. I tightened my grip on his cock, and his head dropped back, his mouth open and wanting, and I gripped harder, pulling with each stroke. As I stroked, his beautiful cock changed color from pink to deep wine, the blood rushing through it. His testicles drew up, just a little, and then he came, gushing big spurts of creamy semen. The first shot splashed up on his chest, and I bent to lick it off. I kept up with a few more strokes and felt his cock soften in my hand.

"Oh, God, that was so good!" His voice was whispery, a little shaky.

"I'll show you good. My turn," I growled.

I turned him around and pushed him against the hay bales. His curved ass had the lightest tan marks above it, white and smooth. My fingers left little grip marks on his flesh as I kneaded his butt, pulling his cheeks apart, then up and down, just playing.

Seeing this beautiful young man bent over, ass thrust out like that, my hard-on straining at my jeans—I couldn't stop.

Sean shifted against me and pressed his butt against my fingers. "Come on. Stop teasing me."

"You got some protection?" I asked him.

"In my jeans. Right front pocket."

I leaned down and fumbled through the fabric, finally finding the lube and condoms. I grabbed the lube and smeared some on my fingers. Sean's ass crack was wine-colored, but the skin outside his hole faded to a rosy pink. A fine layer of fuzz surrounded his anus, golden as the rest of his hair. I circled it with one finger first, just tickling him, letting my cock get more and more worked up.

Sean groaned and pushed backward. "Please!"

"Quit complaining!" I allowed the tease to show in my voice, letting him know I was in charge and loving every second of it. "I'm gonna play as long as I want."

As I slipped one wet finger inside him, he gasped and surged backward, clamping down. He was tight and warm inside, and I wanted to spread him open and dive right in. But I didn't. I made myself go slow.

Owls hooted from the trees, and from a distance I heard a tractor going. All around us the night continued on its normal course of events while I was about to fuck one gorgeous guy.

My cock bonged out of my shorts before I even pulled them down. The air was cool on my hot flesh, and my balls tingled and eased up and down as I freed them. The whisper of the fabric made Sean turn his head. "Oh, man, you've got a helluva cock!" he said.

"Glad you like it." I'm not all that long, maybe seven inches, but I'm thick as a cucumber. I've never gotten any complaints.

"Let me," Sean said. He turned over and sat up, his face flushed and sheened with a light film of sweat. It turned me on even more, seeing him worked up like that. His freckled fingers got a firm grip on my cock, stroking and palming me until I was moaning. He smiled, looking up at me, those gray-blue eyes filled with stormy passion. "You like that?"

"Mmmm-hmmmm," was all I could manage.

My head eased backward as he worked me over, one hand fisted around my cock, the other between my legs. He thrust one finger up behind my balls and rubbed the spot just below my anus. It made me twitch to feel his warm fingers almost inside me, the others wrapped around my aching cock. He thumbed over the precum oozing out of me, making me slick and even harder.

I knew I'd come if I let him keep going. I focused my eyes on him and shook my head. "Time to get down to business."

Sean grinned and kissed me. The condom was wet with lube, and he laughed as he fumbled it over me, stretching the rubber all the way down, tugging it back for a little room at the tip. "Better?" he asked.

"Fucking you will be better. Turn over."

His wet skin made a rubbery, slippery sound against me.

My knees were jammed into the soft hay, and I bent down and nipped at each of his cheeks, smelling his musk, the leftover scent of his semen still on his skin.

I stood up, ready, more than ready. Sean arched his back, making his sweet ass curve against me even more. I spread his cheeks apart, loving the look of him, the feel of his muscular ass in my fingers. I eased inside him with the tip of my cock, going slow, teasing both of us.

"Say it," I commanded.

"Fuck me," he panted back. "Please fuck me!"

I thrust all the way inside him, past the tight band of muscle at his outer ring, then relishing the hotness around my cock. I pushed in as far as I could, my balls rubbing up against his. The trailer shifted as I stroked in and out, the floor squeaking a little as I pumped into him.

I managed to stay on my feet for a few minutes, but as I got closer to coming, I knew I couldn't last. The veins on Sean's neck were pumped up. His face was sweaty and pink. His mouth opened slightly, and he grunted with an "Unh, unh, unh" each time I thrust into him. He somehow managed to spread his legs even more, and he worked his own cock. Seeing his ass move up and down like that really did it for me. He was so beautiful, so horny, so hot. He threw his head back, and I felt his orgasm from inside—the tight spasm of his anus around me, the thrusting spurts of his cock beneath us. He cried out, something long and incoherent and guttural.

I bent over him, nipping on his shoulders, marking him. His skin was wet with sweat and water. He turned his head and managed a kiss on my nose. "Come on, Robby, give it to me. Come inside me, Robby. Fuck me. Fuck me 'til you come!" His voice was husky, dark.

My balls tightened up, swelling with pleasure, and I shot into him with a cry of my own. More than a grunt—nearly a bellow as my lungs whooshed out, the sound thick and hard. My ears buzzed as I came, and I fell onto him, my cock spurting inside him—wet, slippery, and on fire.

Our heavy breathing filled the stall until we finally quieted into a steadier pace. I heard the horses in the paddock and the silly quack of a duck out on the pond. I nuzzled Sean's neck as my cock went completely soft. He turned to kiss me again, one of those awkward half-kisses, and I pulled away reluctantly.

We both stood up and groaned happy groans. Sean smiled and kissed me again, for real this time. I brushed the hay off his damp chest and sticky cock.

It wasn't the usual we-just-fucked-but-man-I-can't-wait-to-get-away-from-you vibe that pops up with strangers. Sean moved slow and soft, comfortable-like as he tugged the condom off me, then pulled my pants all the way off. We sank into the hay, a cool breeze coming through the slats of the trailer.

Sean and I got into it twice more that night. Once on the floor, once up against the wall where he knocked down Bessie's feed bucket as we thrashed our way to coming. Afterward, Sean pulled me down to the soft hay, tugged Bessie's horse blanket over us, sneezed three times, then grinned.

"Maybe you're allergic to horses," I told him.

"Maybe this is worth it," he replied, and pressed more kisses against my neck.

I had a moment's confusion when I woke up. The plastic bucket at my head smelled like grain and horse spit; the blanket smelled of pure horses; and I smelled like sweat and semen. I heard Bessie and Silver Star snorting around in the paddock. I rolled over to peer out at them through the slats, realizing at the same second that the horses were okay, just hungry, and that Sean was gone.

Oh, shit, did I just get played?

I grabbed my jeans and checked the pockets. My wallet was there, intact, nothing taken. The truck keys were in my pocket where I'd left them, the keys to the horse trailer, too. I groaned as I stood up. I was a little old to be sleeping on the floor. My knees creaked as I shook out my legs. The morning air was chilly and misty and made my testicles pull up, my nipples harden.

I measured out the grain into the horses' buckets, feeling foolish. For feeling so left behind. For feeling like Sean was a sweet kid. For wanting him—again.

I gave the mares their buckets and rubbed their necks. The foal suckled while his mama ate her breakfast. After a minute or so, Bessie raised her head and snorted, ears flicking forward. I turned, and from out of the mist I spotted a slender figure clad in dark blue. And then I saw Sean's blond hair.

He was carrying two cups of coffee and had a grin like sunshine on his face.

I smiled back feeling the gray morning turn golden.

ABOUT THE
EDITOR

Johnny Hansen is a ramblin' man who mostly lives in Bakersfield, California. He loves to get out on the open road, crank down the windows, and listen to Loretta Lynn and Waylon Jennings. He also loves the cheap sunglasses, giant Cokes, cowboy hats, and sexy semi-drivin' devils you'll find at truck stops across the country. Drop him a line at truckersex@gmail.com.